Masquerade at Sea House

Other books by Elisabeth Ogilvie

Masquerade at Sea House

by Elisabeth Ogilvie

McGRAW-HILL BOOK COMPANY

New York   Toronto   London   Sydney

Masquerade at Sea House

1

THE TWO came down Cady's wharf in the bright afternoon. Their foreign look was as sharp and sparkling as newly broken glass among the local youngsters eating ice-cream cones while they fished for flounder. Everything about them set them in a world of their own: the boy's haircut, the cut of his suit, his tie and polished shoes, the elegant simplicity of the girl's dark dress, small hat, and white gloves. Their expressions were serious and composed. The boy was about fifteen, tall and thin, with light brown hair and dark eyes, an attractively squarish face with a deep dent in the chin. The girl was slight beside him, but older, her face narrow, delicate, and olive-skinned in contrast with the light brown hair fluffed over forehead and ears.

She led the way down the ramp to the big float where Sam Cady was buying lobsters, waited until the men around the scales became conscious of her, and said politely, "Is it possible to hire somebody to take us out to Sea Island?"

Everyone looked at them with friendly interest. Sam said, "You mean out to the Sanborn place?"

"Yes, sir," said the boy.

"Well, now! Been a long time since any Sanborns went out to Sea Island."

"I'll take you out," said a stout man with white hair

and a red-brown face. "Be on my way home. You young ones expected? The Brices ain't been ashore for a week."

"I think it will be all right," said the girl. "We don't need waiting on, and we'll take food with us. When shall we be ready?"

"Oh, gimme an hour or so. Got to pick up some grub and my mail."

The boy looked at his watch. "We shall be back here at four o'clock, sir. And thank you very much." A formal nod like a bow, and then he smiled at his sister and gestured toward the ramp as if to say, "After you."

A wake of silence followed them up the wharf. When they had disappeared past the store Sam Cady said, "Well, now. I wonder if those are Tom Sanborn's kids."

"Is he the one that eloped with a hired girl, and the grandmother got so mad she closed up the place for good?" a young man asked. "Funny thing, my old man and I were fishing off there the other day and he got to telling me about it. I guess there was works in them days."

"There was works all right," said Sam. "Soured Madam, I can tell ye. She brought up this flock of grandchildren, and I guess she didn't think any of 'em would ever defy her. She never got over the shock." He chuckled. "Madam, they all called her, even her own."

"Funny," mused the white-haired man, "seeing Sanborns going out there again after twenty years or more. I'd just got Garnet Island for myself, and I used to sell 'em lobsters and clams and mackerel, and then all of a

8

sudden one day there's a caretaker there, and the big sign's up, and everybody gone as if they'd never been there. Like it was just a dream I'd had of sailboats and young folks, and the singing coming over the water on quiet nights."

The young man whacked his meaty shoulder. "Cheer up, Gumpy. Might be it's all starting up again with these two, now that the old lady's out of the picture." He looked reflectively up at the wharf. "Show they been brought up foreign, don't they?"

"Ayuh," said Sam Cady. "Tom and his wife run off to Paris. Right after the war, it was. Tom'd been in the Navy."

"Tom Sanborn," Gumpy mused. "Many's the breakfast Tom and the other young folks lost over the side of my boat when I took 'em deep-sea fishing off the Frying Pan Shoal."

At the head of the wharf the boy paid the taxi that had brought them from the airport. Now he and his sister ate ice cream on a stick in a quiet corner of the store.

"Divine," said the girl solemnly. "Absolutely divine."

His curled tongue neatly caught a loose flake of chocolate. "When we went down to that float my stomach didn't think it would ever face ice cream again."

"I told you there was nothing to worry about. If you have an air of knowing exactly what you're about, other people follow right along. You did well, by the way. Too well. I expected you to click your heels and say *Danke schön* or *mille grazie*."

9

They grinned at each other. "Just the same," he said, "I wish we didn't have to wait an hour to escape from here."

"What can happen? Aunt Naomi hasn't the slightest idea that we're at the end of the world, because she hasn't the slightest idea that we left Paris two weeks before she expected us."

"We still have these Brices to convince," he warned her.

"That shouldn't be hard." Her eyes danced in a mock-somber face. "They've never seen any real Sanborns, remember."

"As far as Mrs. Tom knew when she wrote that letter," he said gloomily. He caught the last bite of ice cream before it could drop off the stick. "A whole covey of Sanborns could have dropped in on the place since then. All those western ones, of which we are supposed to be two. Hah!" He laughed with hollow drama.

"That we shall have to chance." His sister was as determined to be gay as he was to be grim.

"Just the same, I'd like to look at that letter once more, and see if there's any minute detail we've missed."

"It's nice to have a family worrier," said the girl, "but you don't have to make it your life work, *cheri*." She patted her handbag. "It's here. Come outside and you can have it."

They went out and sat on their suitcases with their backs against the weathered shingles of the building, the whole glittering, harbor scene dancing vibrantly before them, the scent of salt water in their nostrils, the exciting cries of gulls, and the sounds of engines in their ears.

"It's pure heaven," said the girl. "It's exactly as Father described it, even the waiting here, the expectation of joys to come. They always ate ice cream when they got here, remember? It was better here than anywhere else in the world."

"*The letter*," said her brother. She handed him the envelope, put her head back against the wall, and watched the circling gulls with serene dark eyes. She didn't have to read it with him. She knew it almost by heart.

"Dear Monica and Martin," Mrs. Tom Sanborn had written from New York a month before. "Yesterday by the sheerest coincidence I met your Aunt Naomi in a restaurant—the last time I saw her was years ago—and she gave me the very sad news that your father was gone. She told me also that you would be coming home as soon as your school year ended, but I don't want to wait until then to tell you these things; I think it would be easier on all three of us for me to say on paper, right now, how much your father is involved in some of my happiest memories. Though I have not seen him for years, I have always thought of him and your mother with great affection, and now I feel as if I, too, have lost someone dear.

"Not only was he Tom's closest friend all through their boyhood, but he was best man at our wedding. And then, later, he came to Paris where we were living while Tom studied at the Sorbonne. He met your mother there, and married her.... You were just toddlers when Tom's research work took him in one direction and your father's teaching in another. But we always kept in touch, we always intended to be together

11

again some day, and Mark's and Tom's shared dream was of a summer at Sea House. They were always boys again when they talked of that island. Some day, they said, all hurts would be healed and we'd take our children to Sea House, on Sea Island.

"Well, Tom was first to go, and then your mother; both of them much too young. And now Mark. The estate still isn't settled, and Madam died soon after Tom. Meanwhile the house still stands, watched over by caretakers who know nothing of the family. I always sent Christmas cards and news of Tom to the people who'd looked out for the place for Madam, and then one year I received a note from the Port George postmaster telling me both the old people were gone. New people had been hired, from another part of the coast.

"Because nothing has been decided as to who owns what, none of the family is supposed to use the place, and I don't suppose most of them really care now. It's as if Madam and Sea House were the force that held the clan together, and when she closed it they were all flung violently to the points of the compass. Tom's brother and sister went out to California where an aunt lived, and they both married there; their children can't be expected to cherish a passionate dream about an old house on an island off the Maine coast.

"Tom's Uncle Theo, and a great friend of his, I have never laid eyes on, though he sent us his blessing and a check when we were married. He settled in New Orleans. Occasionally I get a card from him, and the children used to receive little gifts. . . . We can't really blame Ferris,

12

Ferris, Pearn and Abbott for being busy with everything else but the confused Sanborn estate, when the Sanborns themselves seem to have put the whole thing out of mind.

"All but my two Sanborns. They were brought up on their father's homesick dreams, and Simon wants to put things in motion. He plunges straight to the heart of things, and has an idea he can move old Mr. Ferris by sheer vitality. But since he's just enlisted, to put in his Army service before he settles down to his life's work, the estate will just have to wait.

"I shall so look forward to seeing you this summer. Perhaps your aunt will let me show you New York. With Simon in the Army, and Anne a counselor at a camp for handicapped children, I can't think of anything nicer than spending some time with Mark's and Ellen's children. You don't mind my calling you 'children,' do you? Anne and Simon call it my Mother Machree mood, and bear with it gallantly.

Affectionately,
Lydia Sanborn."

Martin Christie sighed. Twenty-four hours ago he had sighed in the same way at Orly as their flight was announced, and the only way of life they had ever known came to an end. Hearing him now in the brilliant light of a Maine summer day, his sister felt a twinge of pain too intense to be borne. No, it didn't do to think about what they had left behind. Besides, if they were lucky they would find their father again, here.

"You see?" she said gaily, taking the letter from him. "We're two of these western cousins. It's very simple."

13

"No, it isn't. We'll be imposters. And if *that's* simple for you, you have a criminal nature."

"We won't be hurting anyone, or stealing anything. Look," she said passionately. "We've never done anything wrong in our lives, in fact we've always been pretty decent and friendly, and helpful whenever we could be. But first we lost our mother, and then our father, and we're going to Aunt Naomi, who loathes us. I know I loathe *her*, sight unseen."

"Does that sound decent, friendly, and helpful?" asked Martin.

"Well, there have to be exceptions to prove the rule.... Father never got his chance to show us Sea House. So we owe this to him, and to us."

Martin pushed out his lower lip and pulled at it. "What if these Brices decide to call New York to see if we have a right to be at Sea House?"

"Then we'll confess we're there without permission, throw ourselves on their mercy, and depart with dignity."

"How dignified can you be after throwing yourself on someone's mercy?" Martin scoffed. But his mouth twitched. They exchanged small, tight grins, and then Monica said, "Let's collect our groceries."

Sea Island lay a few miles southeast of Port George, a long island with thick blue-green spruce woods over a good part of it. As Gumpy's stubby power boat, *Miss Alice,* chugged toward it, the strangers were enchanted by glimpses of sheltered coves and half-hidden meadows

14

brilliant with wild flowers. Monica's heart beat violently. The place was even more beautiful than she'd expected, and from her father's stories she'd imagined it as a Lost Paradise.

Now that the climax of her adventure was about to take place, all the serene courage that had sustained her was suddenly gone, and she felt a little sick. It'll be my fault if anything goes wrong, she thought with a remorseful glance at Martin's entranced face.

Miss Alice entered a small deep cove, passed a white lobster boat on her mooring, and panted up to a spile dock from which a sign warned trespassers off in English, French, and German. "Well, they don't have to be so *firm* about it," Monica said to Martin.

"Madam was most ungracious," said Martin.

A short, broad, flat-bottomed craft painted bright blue and carrying a large outboard motor was tied by the ladder. Back among the spruces sat a small white house with bright flowers around it, and two dogs were racing down toward the wharf. In the silence after the engine was shut off, their barking and the echoes sounded like the outcry of a pack of twenty.

"They ain't vicious," Gumpy explained. "Just noisy and excitable, but you take strangers now, they wouldn't know the difference. Be scared stiff. You get up on the wharf, young feller, and I'll hand up your gear."

Haughtily ignoring the approaching uproar, Martin obeyed. The dogs bounded down the wharf and greeted him like a pair of hysterically friendly wolves. "The Brices got a grandson," Gumpy said. "So the dogs like

15

boys. Hi, Babe. Hi, George." Babe and George rushed to the side of the wharf to salute him, and Monica received a wet kiss as she reached the top of the ladder.

A stout woman was now hurrying down to the landing, flapping her apron as if at hens in her flower garden, calling breathlessly, "You can't land here! You've got the wrong island—look out for the dogs—oh, *dear!*" Red-faced, gasping, she arrived. "Oh, it's you, Gumpy! What in the world—"

"You never did lay eyes on any Sanborns, did ye, Cora?" he asked smugly. "Well, these here are Tom Sanborn's young ones, and I knew Tom real well. Took him fishing all the time." He turned to the other two. "How *is* Tom, by the way?"

Martin became very busy with the dogs. Monica said quietly, "He's dead." Gumpy was shocked.

"You don't say! Why, we never heard nothing about it around here! But then we never hear a dite about the family nowadays, since they don't come any more. Until today." He finished with a pleased chuckle and a duck of his head. Monica's composed smile was a triumph because she had been speaking of her own father, even though Gumpy thought they were speaking of Tom.

Mrs. Brice was at once beaming and fluttering in relief. "Well, of course if Gumpy knows who you are it ought to be all right, even if we never heard you was coming. The estate been settled, has it? Is that why you're here?"

"No, nothing's been settled yet, at least not up until a month ago." Martin was suddenly in charge, smiling

16

into her flushed face. "Mrs. Brice, we don't intend to be a bother. We've brought food, and we thought we could camp out in a couple of rooms at Sea House. We don't expect to be waited on, not in the least."

Mrs. Brice gazed at him with watery admiration. Apparently, like her dogs, she had a fondness for boys. "We've kept the house aired and dry," she said proudly. "Nothing rots out a house like the damp and the dark. Now Elmore's up in the woods cutting firewood, but I can take you over to the house all right."

"Then I guess you're all hunky-dory," Gumpy said. "Cora, you tell Elmore if he wants to help me with the twine we can stop off my cove and get us some nice fat herring to salt down for winter."

"I'll tell him. My!" She marveled all over again. "I was just saying the other day, 'You mark my words, they'll all come down on us one day like a swarm of gulls and say the estate's been settled, and *then* there'll be works around here! A house like that ought to be *used*.'"

"That's right," Gumpy agreed. "It'll be finest kind to see the place teamin' with young ones again." With a final happy chuckle, he started his engine and chugged off.

"Well, I'll show you over to the house," said Mrs. Brice. "You can put your gear on that wheelbarrow. I'll get the key." She started up the slope, talking to herself. Martin's poise vanished at once. He gave his sister a long, tragic look.

"They think we're Simon and Anne! Why didn't you say something?"

17

"Why didn't you?" she retorted. Her heart seemed to be bouncing against the front of her jacket, unpleasantly.

"Oh, no!" He laughed bitterly. "This is your party! Besides, everything went so fast that I was left at the starting gate."

"So was I," she admitted. "And the way she beamed when Gumpy vouched for us, it was like 'Open Sesame!' for us and we were in the cavern full of gems. Oh, come on, Martin!" She squeezed his arm. "Let's go along with it. Simon's in the Army and Anne's at camp, and we deserve a *good* adventure for a change!"

"But we can't get used to answering to those names like *that*." He snapped his fingers.

"We don't have to. Who do you suppose knows the names of Tom Sanborn's children? And if somebody should, which I doubt, we'll tell them we go by our middle names. You do, because there were three Simons at your school. And I do, because a couple of years ago I decided I was tired of plain Anne. Girls are always doing silly things like that. Mrs. Brice might have done it herself, who knows?"

"That's fast thinking," he said sourly, "but look out you don't think us straight into an ambush." Attended by the fervent George and Babe, he loaded the wheelbarrow and started after Mrs. Brice. Monica stood still, just listening. She heard the singing of small birds in the woods, the sudden clatter of crows, the plaintive salute of one gull to another. She smelled grass, flowers, spruce, rockweed, ocean. She felt perfectly secure in this world that glistened like new in its green and gold and blue.

18

Nothing bad could ever happen here. She turned her face to the sky and shut her eyes.

"We're all right, Father," she whispered. "We're fine. So don't worry about us any more."

A wet nose touched her hand. One of the dogs had bounded back to her. "All right, I'll come with you, *caro*," she said.

2

Mrs. BRICE stopped at her house for a key hung from a polished tag of wood marked "Back Door." Sea House was reached by a path that led through a strip of shadowy spruce woods out onto a headland. The place was vast with ells and bays and wings, wide verandas, unexpected little porches, even a tower. Against dark woods, daisy fields, and azure horizon it sprawled in the sun like an amiable many-eyed monster, its gray shingles like scales, its lightning rods like antennae.

"It's magnificent!" cried Martin. "It beats Versailles!"

"It *is* real handsome, isn't it?" said Mrs. Brice.

"*Handsome* isn't strong enough," exclaimed Monica. "Nothing's strong enough. I adore it already. It's just as our father described it only better."

"What about your mother, by the way? She coming later?" asked Mrs. Brice chattily.

"No, she—" Her mind went blank. It was Martin who said, "She can't come. We wanted her to, and she wanted to, but—" He shrugged, his face set in severe, sad lines. Mrs. Brice clucked in pity, then became very hearty as she led the way through a tidy woodshed into a big old-fashioned kitchen. It was ready for use even to a filled woodbox to feed the great black range. There was a large fairly modern refrigerator and a gas stove. Monica made housewifely exclamations, and Mrs. Brice was pleased.

"Yes, it's all set just in case folks should start coming, and I guess they have! I'll show you where the bedding is, and leave you to explore the place and choose your own rooms. My, it must be a real treat for you. It's kind of an ancestral home, isn't it?"

"We think of it that way," Martin said.

"I'll show you where to turn on the gas, and I'll light up the stove for you. Elmore can light up the refrigerator later, that's kind of tricky if you're not used to it." She hustled Martin outside to where the four tall cylinders of bottled gas stood in a martial row against a wall. When they came back in she was calling him Martin, and telling him this would be a real surprise for her grandson. She lit the pilots of the stove for them, talking happily all the while.

"Now if you want anything, you just come and ask me. I've got to scoot now, I got beans in the oven. Come, Babe, George. Oh, I better show you the spring, for drinking water. Elmore's kept it cleaned out."

The spring was a crystal-clear little rock-lined pool, in a path of alders a short way from the woodshed. Tall ferns surrounded it, and the moss was starred with tiny white violets.

It was here that Mrs. Brice left them, gazing at each other with an almost desperate exhilaration.

"Mrs. Brice is ours," Martin said softly.

"Elmore may be difficult," she warned him, but not

really believing it. The assurance she'd felt on the wharf was doubled here. "Let's choose our rooms and make our beds, and then we'll have our first meal in Sea House. Once you eat in a place, you're really there."

"And once you sleep in it," he exulted, "you own it."

He chose a tower room that looked far out to sea. It was reached by its own little staircase, and it held strong traces of an earlier boy; the arrowhead and rock collections, the model schooner, the pictures and school banners, a drawer full of slacks and jerseys, sneakers and boots in the closet.

Monica's room was large, square, full of light, with gracefully simple furniture painted white. It had long windows and one deep window seat, curtained and cushioned in faded rose. More roses bloomed dimly from the hooked rugs laid over straw matting. Framed photographs yellowed with time hung in clusters against the faintly flowered wallpaper. There were also a number of amateur water colors and pencil sketches of island scenes, dated and initialed. There was no clothing here, but the empty drawers held a ghostly fragrance.

They changed their formal clothes for shorts and sneakers, and met for the tour. The rest of the house was unbelievable for two who had spent their years living in so many places, always transients, never belonging. A family had lived continuously here through many generations, and when Tom Sanborn's grandmother had decided in her rage to leave, the house had been closed and kept just as it was in that moment.

"It'll take us weeks to see everything," Monica marveled. "I don't even know where to start. The attic? The parlors? All the miles of cupboard and closets?"

"Full of dried corpses, probably," said Martin. "What about the cellar? In our foolishness we'll probably lift a trap door and let out the Sanborn Monster."

Monica giggled, feeling young and happy for the first time in months. They were in the ballroom that took up half the second story, its polished floor gleaming through a film of dust. Martin ran up some scales on the big square piano. "Out of tune but a good instrument," he said professionally and began to play a Chopin waltz. Monica kicked off her sneakers and did a chain of *tours jettés* down the room. He went on playing and she went on dancing, intent and joyous. Being slightly off key and played in an empty house, the music had a wistful gaiety as if it were a waltz for a ghost and she was that ghost—

She stood still her heart hammering and not from exertion. Martin stopped and looked at her, and she made herself laugh. "I'm starving!"

"I thought from your expression that you saw the sheriff coming through the pass. I'm starving too."

They got supper together. They had been dependent upon each other for most of their lives, ever since their mother died and their father had become increasingly withdrawn, giving up the teaching of English for the more solitary work of writing and translating. They had lived in many different places, picking up languages as they prowled about their new locations like a couple of adventurous young cats. They always found out at once where to buy bread and milk, eggs from a local farmer, fish from the local fishermen; they became acquainted with far more people than their father ever suspected. Sometimes Martin traveled with a crowd of neighborhood boys and was lost to Monica for a while, or she was drawn into a circle of schoolmates. But always their relationship was as fundamental as breathing, that of two persons who, beneath everything else, know they have only each other in the whole world.

Now Monica made an omelet and Martin a salad, and they carried their trays outside to the flat granite ledges surrounded by a garden gone wild. They had a view of the eastern sea across fragrant thickets of big loose-petaled red and white roses. Birds sang from the woods and moved freely in the garden. It was a tranquil hour, deep gold from the setting sun, blue with long shadows.

"I wonder what Father would say if he could see us now" said Monica.

"I wonder if I've picked out his room . . . You know, from up there you can see a good sand beach, and there's a building that may be a boathouse—" He broke off as the dogs burst from the woods, terribly glad to see them again. Laughing, holding their plates out of reach, the two didn't see the man and boy until they were close enough to speak.

The man was slight and wiry, his eyes narrow under jutting brows and black in his dark-burnt face, his nose like the prow of a ship. The boy drifted behind him, hands in his pockets, his T-shirt tight over broad chest and shoulders, his crewcut like yellow plush.

Martin got up at once and went down over the ledge. "Are you Mr. Brice, sir?" he asked respectfully, putting out his hand.

"Ayuh. And you're a couple of Sanborns. Wife can't talk about anything else." He didn't smile as they shook hands. "This feller here is Homer Brice, my grandson."

"Hi," said Homer indifferently, without taking his hands from his pockets. He was good-looking in a ruddy, snub-nosed way, and Monica suspected that he was vain about his build.

"This is quite a surprise," Mr. Brice said. "We never got no word from the lawyers that you was coming."

Monica joined the group, smiling, but not too much. He might distrust that. "It was something that happened too fast, I think. It was decided all at once. We arrived unexpectedly from Paris and nobody in the family was ready for us. Since we'd never been here, it seemed a good idea to put us on a plane for Maine so we could see the place. You can write to the trustees if there's any doubt."

Mr. Brice pulled hard at his long jaw. "Wife says you figger to look after yourself."

"Oh, we do," Monica assured him. "We won't be any trouble, and we're careful about fire and things like that."

"Well." Mr. Brice looked out to sea. "I guess it must be all right. I s'pose there's no reason why Sanborns shouldn't start coming . . . Better light up that icebox while I'm here."

It seemed the polite thing to go in with him and watch

25

in respectful silence until he had the burner silently and efficiently working. Homer remained outside, standing on a ledge like a monument and gazing out to sea.

"There, that'll start to get cold right off," said Mr. Brice. "I'll get home to my baked beans. Wife says to ask you over." He did not seem enthusiastic.

"Please thank her for us," said Monica, "but we've already eaten. And thank you for starting the refrigerator."

He nodded and turned to go, with a word to the dogs. As they entered the woods path he was talking to them, which proved that he could smile. Homer, hands still in pockets, gave a long look back at the two on the ledge and then followed Mr. Brice.

"Compared to Homer, Babe and George scintillate," remarked Monica.

"Is it human? Or is it the Robot that walks like a Man?" asked Martin in sepulchral tones. "And what if Mr. Brice has second thoughts and writes to New York?"

"Then we leave," said Monica calmly. "But somehow I feel that he's accepting us as a natural phenomenon like fog or thunderstorms." She lay back on the warm ledge, her arms under her head, and watched three gulls flying over with wings washed gold by the sunset.

Martin was reassured by her confidence, as always. "Come on, let's see if that's a boathouse."

They went down through bayberry, juniper, daisies, and buttercups, to find a pretty little half-moon sand beach. At one end stood a small weathered building with swallows nesting under its eaves. They filled the golden air with chatterings and beating wings as the two human beings approached.

The place was locked, but they shaded their eyes and looked in at the window. In the shadows they saw a slim light dory, looking graceful even out of water; a stubby little skiff; and a sailing dinghy whose mast and tightly furled red sail were suspended from the peak of the roof.

"A-*ha!*" said Martin.

"You'll sail alone, my boy," said his sister. "Anyway, that sail's probably rotten by now."

"I don't like your attitude. It's negative, and if there's one thing we must—not—*be,* it's negative."

"Um." Monica yawned till her eyes watered. "I'm thinking positively about bed. It's been two hundred years since this morning."

"And yesterday morning we woke up in Paris," said Martin. "Awe-inspiring, what?"

3

W HEN MONICA woke suddenly it was still night. She thought she was in the little cramped room in Paris, and tried to make the long pale shapes of the windows fit the idea. Then she remembered, stretched, sniffed at the blend of salt water and roses coming in, and thought blissfully, Here we are. We did it. There were some bad moments, but I didn't let Martin know I was afraid. And if he worried, he kept it from me. Most of the time, anyway . . .

There was a sound. Whether it was far off in the house or close by, she couldn't tell, only that there was a soft stirring, a little thump now and then, something like footsteps felt, not heard . . . Was it the beating of her own pulses? She remembered joking with Martin about the Sanborn Monster. What if Something did live in the house? There were places in England that were haunted; the most reputable people swore to it.

"Oh, don't be so silly," she whispered to herself, but just the same she wished they'd picked out rooms nearer together. Martin was off there in his tower, probably sleeping so hard it would take a shotgun explosion to wake him.

Where *were* those noises? Overhead? In the next room? Downstairs? *On* the stairs? They seemed to be everywhere. She sat up, willing her teeth not to chatter,

28

reaching a shaky hand for her robe. Should she lock her door and windows and stay put, or try to get to Martin? That meant going through miles of passages with only a flickering candle to light the way, because they'd never thought about flashlights.

That rustling was definitely in the hall near her door, and would she get it locked in time? Did she dare to move? You are an idiot, she told herself scornfully, to panic now after the cable-car accident in Switzerland, and the homicidal maniac who ran wild that time in Italy, and the drunken *concierge* in Paris . . . But I could *see* all those things, she argued. They weren't bumps and scrapes and slitherings in a huge old house that nobody's lived in for twenty years, on an island, in pitch-black night.

And now she realized that her door was slowly swinging open on the dark gulf of the passage outside. She was too stunned even to feel horror as a shapeless mass rustled through the opening and emitted a strange low sound.

"Are you awake?"

She sagged back giddy with relief and hissed, "Shut that door! Did you hear anything?"

"What do you think I'm doing down here?" Martin whispered back. The key turned in the lock, and Monica scrabbled for matches. She lit her candle in its old-fashioned holder, and saw Martin swathed in a brilliant quilt.

"Joseph and the coat of many colors," she said.

"It's not funny," he said with dignity. He settled himself on the foot of the bed, well wrapped. "You should

29

have heard what woke me up. Moaning, something dragging, noises in the walls. What did *you* hear?"

"I can't describe it exactly, but it sounded like all kinds of horrors straight out of that favorite book of yours, *Tales of the Supernatural*." They listened again, but there was only silence, as thick and intense as black velvet. "It could have been squirrels," she suggested.

"Moaning?"

"That could have been a little breeze blowing over a hole somewhere or a drainpipe."

"What breeze?" Martin was skeptical. "There's not a breath of air stirring." Just then a faint wisp of wind made the candle flame shiver, and she said, "You see?"

He pushed out his lower lip and shrugged. "But I'm not going back along those five miles of black tunnel. Did you ever realize what sheer horror an ordinary closed door can suggest? And one that clicks open as you pass it can send you straight up through the ceiling. It almost did me."

Monica laughed. "Be my guest. There's the sofa, and you can have one of my pillows."

When they were settled down, the candle blown out, and Monica composing herself for sleep, Martin said, "Do you think we did the right thing coming here?"

She felt a little clutch of dismay, but said dryly, "What's the matter, do you think it's your conscience making all those weird noises?"

"Be honest about it. How do you feel?"

"I feel we've done the right thing for *us*." She could be joyfully honest. "Nobody else in the world—and especially Aunt Naomi—would think it was right, but we do. Besides, why did everything go off so well if it weren't meant to happen? The airplane for Maine was right there, there were two last-minute cancellations, and when we got to Port George and asked how we could get out here, nobody questioned us. And the Brices have accepted us."

"It's a good thing this family has a worrier," Martin said grimly. "Me. You'd walk a tightrope across the Alps if anybody dared you."

"You mean you want to be safe and snug with Aunt Naomi?"

"*No!*" he exploded. "The trouble is, it's so perfect here that if we do get thrown out I'll probably drown myself off the wharf. I wish we could stay forever. It's not fair for us to have to be at the mercy of somebody who hated our mother and thinks we should never have been born."

Unexpectedly Monica's throat tightened. They'd been carried on first by their exhilaration and daring, and then by the beauty of this new world. But what Martin said was the bleak, uncompromising truth. Because they were under twenty-one, they were helpless. Aunt Naomi *had* hated their mother; whenever she wrote to their father she had never mentioned either his wife or the children, as if by ignoring them she could make them cease to exist. But their father, certain of her integrity under her bitter shell, had made her their guardian. Of course he hadn't really expected they'd ever need a guardian; death had come as a surprise, long before it should have been due.

Oh, Father! Monica cried silently to him now. If we

31

couldn't have you, why couldn't it be somebody else? Even a bank would be better than Aunt Naomi!

Martin was talking. "In the old days people could lose themselves. They set out to seek their fortunes and nobody bothered them. Now it's police and the FBI, and television, and radio, so there's no place left to hide, nowhere in the world."

"We're pretty well hidden here."

"For how long? The day we're supposed to arrive, she'll check Paris and find out when we left. At Kennedy they'll know who came in and went out on what planes that day, and they'll trace us to Augusta and the taxi, and there you are. She'll know for sure we were born with criminal natures, and ship us off to schools for delinquents until we're twenty-one. Welcome to Pleasantview Concentration Camp."

"Well, that will be a nice change from Aunt Naomi," said Monica. "Listen, you've admitted yourself that nobody will start checking until two weeks from now, unless by some absolutely fantastic coincidence some of the family decide to visit here. And we're used to living a day at a time, you know that. So stop worrying. I know it's your profession, but you're on holiday now."

There was a reluctant chuckle from the sofa, a shifting and creaking. "All right. But I'm not wasting any time getting that sailboat overboard." He yawned loudly. "Good night, Anne-Monica."

"Good night, Simon-Martin."

4

THE DAWN CHORUS of songbirds, the morning cries of gulls flying in from their nesting ledges, lobster boats passing among the islands on their way to outside fishing grounds—these were all real. The terrors of the night, the doubts and self-searchings, vanished before the dazzling fact of a field of daisies, a sapphire sea, and the fascination of Sea House.

The brother and sister ate a very early breakfast on the broad front veranda where honeysuckle twined with tropical splendor and fragrance. "What are you going to do first?" Martin asked.

"Dishes and beds."

He looked pained. "You don't have to do those things till you're ready."

"I'm ready now. It would take only about two days for this house to begin to look like a gypsy camp without the guitars and earrings."

"I wanted to get the sailboat out," he said sadly.

"Well, go and get the key, and I'll be along as soon as I do my little housewifely chores."

"Leave my bed for me to make, and I'll wipe the dishes—" But he already had one leg over the railing.

She laughed. "I don't need you! Hurry up!" She looked affectionately after him as he ran through the wild garden, his long-legged shadow leaping with him. He

33

was a worrier, and she liked seeing him fervent about having fun with the sailboat. Contentedly she washed the dishes from last night and this morning, enjoying the soft rain water pumped from the cistern. She made Martin's bed in spite of his orders, lost herself for a little while in the view from his tower, examined the boy's possessions in the room. When she went downstairs he wasn't back with the key yet, so she stole the chance for a little exploring.

The dining room's bay windows framed field, woods, a bit of blue water, and the eastern tip of Gumpy's island. A beautiful oil lamp hung on adjustable chains from the ceiling over the long table. One wall was entirely composed of glassed-in shelves full of dishes, and drawers below where linens were stored. She hesitated to handle them, they'd been so carefully laid away, but she could examine the dishes without touching them. One green and white set of fine china with an ornate yet delicate decoration kept drawing her eye. She and Martin had been using the sturdy ironstone ware in the kitchen cupboard, but she was determined that they should have at least one meal on this lovely china, at this table, in the soft yellow light of the hanging lamp. That is, they'd have it if she dared to handle the fragile stuff. One chip off a cup would be a chip off her heart.

As she returned to the big hall, where the front door stood open to the morning, Martin's whistle pierced the quiet. It was their own signal; "The call of the mysterious and almost extinct bulb-nosed moppet," Martin used to explain it solemnly.

34

She whistled in answer and ran down to the beach, met by cavorting dogs. The bright blue outboard skiff was pulled up on the sand, and Homer was in the boathouse with Martin, tying new rope to an anchor. The dinghy had already been moved out on rollers. Her name was *Undine*.

"Homer brought me around with the speed of light, practically," said Martin. "No wonder he calls her *The Blue Streak*."

"Yep, she can sure travel," said Homer with a fond glance toward the outboard skiff. He gave Monica a grin that quite changed his face. "How'd you sleep your first night on the island?"

"It was the best night's sleep in months," she said, honestly forgetting the few frightening moments.

"We don't need you to pull," Martin told her, "but I wanted you to see the launching. Homer doesn't think she'll fill and sink within five minutes."

"No, she's pretty tight. Well, I guess the tide's as high as it's going to be, so let's get her going."

Undine slid over the rollers down across the sand and into the water, the boys splashing barefoot beside her. Monica cheered and clapped, and the dogs barked. Homer climbed aboard his boat, started the engine, and towed the dinghy out into the cove and anchored her. Then he came ashore and said, "Now let's get the skiff and the dory out, and you'll be all set."

With these perched above high water mark, they all three sat on the sand, and Martin smiled tenderly at *Undine*. "I'll bet she skims like a bird."

35

"For my money I'd rather have that dory with a good outboard motor," said Homer.

"Don't you like to sail?" Martin was incredulous. "With all this water to yourself?"

"Nope. I like engines. This one's a ten-horse. I'm saving for a twenty-five, and then watch me go. Of course I'll have to have me a bigger boat."

"Canvas for me, every time," said Martin.

"I can see the point of getting somewhere fast," Monica said, wanting to please Homer because he was being so friendly. "Sailing is—well, just the act of sailing. It's a thing in itself, I guess you'd say."

"Sure!" Homer nodded emphatically. "For me, a boat's to take me from one place to another, like a car. And I want to get there fast, no lallygagging."

"Then you really enjoy the sensation of speed for it's own sake," argued Martin. "Admit it."

For someone who could look so stolid, Homer was really attractive when he smiled, and Monica felt even more pleased with herself and the place. "Okay, I admit it. Speed's everything. There's nothing like tearing out of the harbor with the whole ocean ahead of you, and you feel like heading straight out to sea and never stopping. Except that you can't carry enough gas with you," he added. "Boy, wouldn't I like to fly one of those big jets that go over here on the way to Gander."

"How do you get to be one of those pilots?" Monica asked him, and he looked blank, shrugged, and said, "I dunno."

"Now for a little breeze," said Martin, "and I'll take my girl out."

"We can get a darn good southwest breeze in the afternoons, and you'll know you aren't on some tame little French river. So don't go taking any foolish chances."

"I won't. I'm the cautious kind."

"He's the family worrier," said Monica. "It saves me a lot of work."

Homer lay back with his arms folded under his head and looked up into Monica's face. "So you slept good, did you?" His eyes were sparkling blue slits. "Sure you didn't hear any old bones rattling?"

"Should I have?"

"Some folks've heard 'em."

"Some folks must have a pretty powerful imagination," said Martin, flopping onto his stomach.

"What would you say if I told you I'd heard something?"

"Squirrels," suggested Monica.

"There aren't any squirrels on the island. It's too far out for any kind of wild animals. Nope, I heard things I couldn't put a name to, and I don't scare easy."

Monica felt a delicate chill along her spine. She didn't look at her brother. "Did they scare you?" Martin asked casually.

"They scared me right out of the house in the middle of the night. The woods were some black and I'd gone kiting out without my flashlight, but I felt a lot safer than I did in that place." He raised up on one elbow. "See, I'd had this bee in my bonnet about sleeping in the house, and finally Gramp told me I could. Well, that bee got finished off quick, I can tell you."

"What kind of sounds were they?" Monica asked.

37

"Crashes first, like somebody falling into a pile of dishes. Sliding and thumping like a body being dragged downstairs. You'd have sworn there was a murder going on," he said earnestly. "When I got back home and woke Gramp up, he took his shotgun and called the dogs and came over here. The dogs range at night," he explained, "so nobody can land on the island after dark and get into the house. There's a lot of stuff in there could be stolen. All the old lady took off was her silver. She used to lug it back and forth from New York each year."

"You don't think somebody could have got by the dogs and into the house, do you?" asked Martin. "They can't be everywhere at once, and—"

"There wasn't a sign of anything moved or broken inside the house, no footprints anywhere. The dogs never got excited around the place at all. So what do you think of *that?*"

"I don't know." Monica managed a feeble smile.

"Well, I know what I think, and so does Gramp, but he won't admit it."

"You mean the place is haunted?" Martin inquired.

"You can laugh if you want to."

"I'm not laughing. I've heard of haunted houses before. But who's haunting it?"

"The old lady, maybe. Or somebody before that. There used to be settlers on all these islands and they were killed by Indians. Might be some feller from way back is rattling around here at night wondering where his cabin went to."

Monica laughed. "Well, in that case I'm not going to

38

be afraid of him. I'll make him a cup of tea and be friends."

"I'd like to see that tea party." Homer grinned. "Him sitting around in his bones . . . But Gramp had a queer time over here once, too. That's why he seemed pretty stuffy about you staying in the house, but he didn't want to scare you if there was no need. He was out after herring with Gumpy one night, and when he was rowing home he saw a light in the house."

Monica's breakfast pancakes seemed unusually heavy in her stomach. "Flickering, I suppose?" she said mockingly.

"Seemed to be moving from one room to another. So he rowed in to the beach here and went up to the house, but it disappeared. Babe came up to him and she wasn't worked up at all. And those dogs really whoop it up when they come across a stranger's tracks."

"Maybe it wasn't a stranger," said Martin.

"It wasn't anybody," said Homer somberly. "Not anybody the dogs could smell. But if you haven't heard anything, might be they've stopped coming." He got up and stretched toward the sky. "Time I was taking off instead of laying around telling ghost stories."

"Do you live with your grandfather?" Martin asked.

"Sometimes. I'm back and forth between here and the Port. Depends on what I pick up for jobs."

"When do you want to go for a sail with me?"

They both laughed at that. "You show me some speed in that thing without tipping us out, and I'll believe there's something to it." He looked down at Monica

39

with his bright blue crinkling smile. "I'll see you again."

"Come and eat with us," Martin invited. "Monica's a good cook."

"I bet she is." He went down to *The Blue Streak,* pushed it off and swung himself in. He poled himself out for a little way with an oar, and then started the engine. As it idled throatily he waved back at them, then turned up the throttle and shot out of the cove with a tremendous roar and a swashing wake that made waves on the shore. The dogs barked him away, then came running to the two on the sand.

"I take back what I thought last night," said Martin, scratching George's ears. "He's all right. Maybe Gramp squelches him."

"I didn't care much for his stories though, especially where we did hear something. And he says there aren't any squirrels."

"Do you think the place is really haunted?"

She shrugged and jumped up. "I don't know. It won't be dark for at least twelve hours so let's just forget it and take a walk around the shore."

"Right." He gave a loving glance back at *Undine.* "Don't you like her? I'll bet she sails like a dream. The sail's not rotten, by the way."

"That's delightful," said his sister, "but I expect you to wear a life-preserver. I saw some in the boathouse."

She laughed at his martyred groan.

5

THEIR MORNING WALK eventually brought them out at the Brice house, where Mrs. Brice offered them cold milk and fresh cake. She suggested that Martin wheel home a five-gallon can of kerosene for the lamps.

Monica filled two and expertly trimmed the wicks. Tonight they'd be able to read in bed, if they could stay awake long enough. These chores done, they dug clams at low tide in one little cove, and had them for lunch. Then Monica went beachcombing while Martin took *Undine* out for several hours' sailing among the islands in a light breeze. He met Gumpy, who gave him two lobsters for their supper.

"I asked him if he remembered a Mark Christie," Martin reported, "and he wasn't sure until I told him about Father getting the big halibut that time. Then he remembered him, how excited he was thinking he'd hooked a whale, and how hard he laughed at things, and how he was always singing 'On Top of Old Smokey' and making up new words for it about everything that went on."

They looked at each other in somber pleasure. Their father had come alive for them in this place all at once, because somebody else remembered him.

There were no sounds to waken them that night. They woke to fog and a gentle rain, and ate breakfast in the kitchen, warmed by a crackling wood fire in the big black range. After the chores were done they went up the narrow flight of stairs that led to the attic from the front of the house. Martin had already been up the back stairs, which went up between the kitchen and the wood-shed, but the door at the top was fastened with a padlock. The door at the head of the front staircase was merely hooked, and as they wandered through the rooms under the roof Monica remembered their father's accounts of hair-raising hide-and-seek up here on stormy nights, while the older people sat by the fire in the living room with their books, needlework, and chess games.

It must have been nice, she thought wistfully, picking up a Teddy bear in the playroom. So many in the family and of all ages. And now, who remembers? We do, but it's second-hand and we're not Sanborns.

Two more rooms, furnished with worn but comfort-able old things, must have been used as clubrooms; they could tell which had been the boys' lair and in which one past generations of girls had talked away rainy hours. The main room of the attic had a billiard table, and Martin and Monica played a game, enjoying the sound of the rain so close to their heads. Leaving there, they glanced into a dim chamber under the eaves, filled with trunks and cartons, and then came to a door that was fas-tened with a padlock, like the one at the top of the back stairs.

"I wonder what they've got hidden in there." Martin tried to shake the door, but it was solid. "The Brices must have the key."

"And they can keep it. After all, it's really none of our business."

"But there may be real treasure in that room."

"What are you going to do with it?" she teased him. "Steal it and make your fortune?"

"But look at everything else they've left out in the open, they were so sure everybody would pay attention to the signs. So what could they possibly want to hide away like this?"

"The Sanborn Monster? . . . Oh, family papers, perhaps," Monica suggested. "Things that had a special sentimental value for Madam. It doesn't have to make any sense, whatever it is. She was the head of the family and could afford to indulge her whims."

"I'd like to reach that high elevation sometime. I'd indulge in some whims regarding Aunt Naomi."

"Get that lethal glint out of your eye, *mon frère*, and don't brood about that door. Remember what happened to Bluebeard's wife."

"Sister Anne, Sister Anne, what do you see?" he whined in falsetto. They went away from the door laughing, but he looked back once at it, and when they got downstairs he said, "I wonder if that other locked door goes into the same room."

"Maybe. Let's go out, it's stopped raining."

They found boots to fit them in the collection in the woodshed and went out into the hushed warm fog, scented with sea and flowers. Foghorns seemed to ask questions and answer them, and they heard the deep warning voice of a vessel feeling her way up the coast.

43

"Shore or woods?" asked Monica.

"Shore for me. If you get off the trail in the woods you could wander in circles all day."

"You can't really get lost on this place," she scoffed. "I'm for the woods."

"If you get confused, start whistling and I'll come and find you," said Martin kindly.

"I'll probably get Babe and George instead, and we'll all have to go find you," she retorted. She set out along the path that led to the woods seen yesterday from the dining room. In a few minutes she was surrounded by fog. She smiled in pleasure at her solitude.

The track through them was edged with bright green sprays of fern and tangles of climbing blackberry blossoms. Beyond the pure white petals lay the resin-scented shadow, where the sudden flight of a bright-colored wood warbler turned the bird into a shooting star in a night sky. She came to a fork, and took the branch which should lead northwards. She wandered on, enchanted by nature's arrangement of mossy boulders and tiny blossoming plants and clusters of vivid mushrooms —one day soon she must pick some of the edible ones she recognized, with a happy start of surprise, from French woods.

The fog drifted lazily among the trees and dripped like gentle rain from the boughs. She wasn't wearing her watch, so she didn't know how long she had been walking, looking, and listening when she began to feel very sodden around the legs of her slacks. And *hungry*. The

44

hearty breakfast was a dim memory. It was time to go home, but when she turned to go back, nothing looked the same.

"All right, brother mine," she said aloud, "take that smug grin off your face." She sat down on a rock and listened for the surge on the shore, but the sea was flat calm today. The distance-muted foghorns seemed to sound from everywhere. "Well, if I walk straight in one direction I'm bound to get out of the woods sometime," she observed. "That is, if I can keep going in a straight line. At least if the dogs have to find me *they* won't say, 'I told you so.'"

She started on again, thought she recognized a certain golden-orange toadstool, and then had to climb over a moss-draped fallen tree she'd never seen before. The woods grew darker as the fog grew more dense, and she thought she heard a far-off rumble of thunder. Her stomach tightened. There could be harm in any woods, if you were caught in them during a thunder storm.

Finally she had to give in and whistle. It echoed weirdly through the trees. She whistled again, waited. The third whistle was answered, and there was no doubt of the direction of the answer. She whistled as she started toward the signal, which continued to come with reassuring regularity. The way was rough, over blow-downs, but at last the woods began to thin out, and the ground slanted sharply up toward a fringe of old wind-stunted spruces, and the whistle came from there.

Suddenly it broke off, there was a choking cry, and a large splash. An invisible fist squeezed her stomach but

45

not her legs. She raced up over the slippery spruce spills, crying her brother's name. At the crest of the rise she came to a sickening stop, gripping a spruce bough just over her head. The land had been so worn away from the narrow cliff that the very ground under her feet seemed to rest on air. Below it there would have been nothing to break her fall to the jagged black ledges around which today's calm sea lay quietly.

Her stomach heaving, she took a few cautious steps backward. There was no sign of Martin, and if he'd been there and fallen he would still be in sight—though quite possibly a broken and unconscious Martin, already drowned if he lay face down. The only thing in sight below was a wormy old log, floating.

She wanted to sit down, but she had to keep moving and not give in to the way she felt. At least she was at the shore now, and she'd have to arrive eventually at the Brices' landing or at the boathouse beach.

She went along the edge of the small cliff until the ground solidified into the usual juniper-bayberry-ledge mixture, and then down onto the big rocks close to the water. She tried to whistle again, but her mouth was too dry. Sweating now, she hurried around a massive jumble of yellow boulders and saw Homer Brice, hands on hips, scowling around him. When he saw her he shouted, "Hey, was that you whistling?"

"Yes, but I was answering Martin!" Her words fell over one another. "And now I can't find him. Have you seen him?"

"Heck no, I was looking for him, or you, whoever it was. You can get lost in the fog on this place."

46

"I wasn't worried about that, but I did almost go head-first over the cliff back there." She sat down abruptly because her knees were weak. Homer sat down too, and kindly offered her a stick of gum. She didn't ordinarily like it, but this time it offered restorative possibilities.

"You better be careful," Homer warned her. "Don't go chasing through the woods alone."

"I was enjoying myself till I thought I heard thunder."

"Yep, it was kind of muttering around there for a while, but I guess it went up by to the north."

The war cry of the bulb-nosed moppet shrilled from behind a fog-wreathed point, and Homer put two fingers in his mouth and whistled a blast in return. Martin appeared, rumpled, wet, and cross.

"So this is where you are, while I've been all around Robin Hood's barn chasing up your signal." He glared at his sister.

"I've been chasing yours," she retorted. "And it wasn't easy. Why didn't you stay in one place? I had you bashed to pieces on the rocks, drowned, or—"

Martin, flushed, opened his mouth, and Homer laughed. "Don't fight, fellers. Blame it on the woods and the water. They carry sounds in some mighty queer ways. Sit down, Martin, and have a stick of gum."

Martin continued to glare at his sister. "Did you or did you not let out one shriek as if the Sanborn Monster had just grabbed you?"

"I did not shriek. But I heard you choke as if the Monster had you by the throat in mid-whistle."

"What's this about the Sanborn Monster?" Homer's blue eyes darted from one to the other. Monica started to laugh, ready to explain, but Martin spoke solemnly.

"I shouldn't have mentioned it. In fact I shouldn't even *know* about it until I'm twenty-one, and Monica shouldn't know about it at all. We heard about it by accident."

"About *what*, for Pete's sake?" Homer was tense.

"Well, it's something they tell the males of the family when they get to be twenty-one. The family secret, curse, horror, whatever you want to call it. It's existed for hundreds of years. The first Sanborn to come to America brought the curse with him, to his sorrow, because he thought he was escaping it and saving his heirs from it for good."

"Aw, I've heard of curses," said Homer with contempt. "What's with this monster bit?"

"Oh, nobody's really *believed* in the Monster for years," Monica assured him. "Except when something happens that nobody can figure out, like the time one Sanborn disappeared out of a locked room one night and was never found. And there was another one who, all at once, began keeping the lights on all night, and did so for the rest of his life without ever telling why."

"That's a tame story when you consider the one who was found all bitten up one morning—dead, of course," Martin contributed. "There wasn't an expert who could identify the toothmarks. Gruesome, isn't it? Still gives me chills. But most of us just laugh about it."

Homer's smile was thin. "Well, it wasn't any monster screeching and choking around here today. Most likely blackback gulls or a blue heron." He got up. "Gramp's looking for me to help work up firewood. And Grammy wants you fellers to come to supper tonight. Ha'past five."

"We were going to ask you to have supper with us," said Monica on the spur of the moment. "Can you come tomorrow night?"

"I sure can." He gave her his wide and likable grin. "So long, both of you, and you better keep to the shore going back."

When he had gone around the point Monica said, "I think we got back at him a bit for his stories, don't you? Maybe we should start writing thrillers."

"I suppose you didn't mind getting lost," Martin said, straight-faced, "if Homer was the one to find you."

"I found him." She told him her experience, and he told her his.

"I did almost fall, but I didn't yell, I was too startled. And it was a good way from here. There was an old well in a little clearing, near a cellar hole. It had a fairly new wooden cover, good and stout, probably to keep the dogs from falling in. Well, somehow the cover had got dislodged, and if you couldn't see that, you wouldn't even know there was a hole in the ground. I fell over some rocks and nearly went headfirst down the well."

She listened quietly, as if that fist weren't squeezing her stomach again. If he *had* fallen—

"Anyway," he went on, "I discovered the cover in the alders, and put it back on, and laid the rocks on it. I think they belonged on it."

"How could they have got moved, and the cover? Do

49

you suppose there's someone else on here? Or some big animal that they don't know about, like a bear?" She couldn't help glancing over her shoulder fearfully. "It could swim out here, couldn't it?"

He laughed at her. "If you don't sound like a city bird! What I think is that either Homer or Mr. Brice himself moved the the cover to get some water when they were sawing down some trees nearby, and then something interrupted them before they got the top back on, and they never thought of it again. Remind me to mention it to Mr. Brice tonight."

She showed him the cliff where she'd almost fallen. A pair of big blackback gulls rode the gentle swell offshore. "I suppose it was one of those I heard," she said. "Well, at least we've got a logical explanation for these noises, if not for the ones in the house."

"Oh, there's probably a logical reason for those too," said Martin loftily. "Natural causes. Wind, the house settling, so forth and so on."

"And the Sanborn Monster," said Monica. "Locked in the attic biding his time. And do you realize we haven't been down to the cellar yet?"

"Probably his mate lives down there," said Martin. "The Monstress."

6

SUPPER AT THE Brices' consisted of lobster chowder, the first that Monica and Martin had ever tasted, and they found it as wonderful as their father had promised them. There was a crisp green salad; there were hot biscuits and homemade jams and jellies and pickles. For dessert there was warm wild-strawberry pie. Mrs. Brice was flustered, as usual, but they'd come to know that she was really warm and maternal. Mr. Brice had little to say, and answered their attempts at conversation with "Ayuh?" or worse, "That so?" However, Homer was talkative, and the dogs were extremely sociable.

Fondling Babe's ears Monica said, "Maybe if I'd had you with me this morning I wouldn't have got lost."

"You can take either of 'em with you whenever you've a mind to," Mrs. Brice assured her.

"That reminds me," said Martin, and he told Mr. Brice about the well. This time he got more than "That so?" Mr. Brice became alert and suspicious.

"You sure you didn't knock the lid off when you fell against it?"

"I'm sure, because it was in the alders on the other side." Martin politely stood his ground. "I'd have seen it if it had been in place. Anyway, it'll take a good strong heave to dislodge it now, because I piled on all the rocks I could find around there."

51

Homer grinned. "We keep it covered because the old gink who used to have a cabin up that way drowned in the well, and nobody ever bothered to get him out. We don't want his skeleton climbing out and dancing around in the moonlight."

"*Homer!*" gasped his grandmother. "You stop those lies!"

"Oh, that doesn't scare them any. You ought to hear them tell about the Sanborn Monster that lives in the attic."

"I never heard tell of such foolishness." Mrs. Brice looked reproachfully at them. "I don't know how you can sleep nights."

Martin discovered the cottage organ in the corner of the sitting room. "May I play it?" he asked Mr. Brice, who nodded and went back to leafing through a mail order catalog. Martin tried a few chords, getting the knack of pumping with his feet and playing at the same time. Then he tried out the variety of stops, and began to play hymns from the open book on the music rack.

The others were drawn to that corner like bees to a rosebush, and Mr. Brice put down his catalog and sat listening, pipe in his mouth and deep-set eyes watching Martin's every move. Mrs. Brice started to sing in a true, youthful voice, Homer joined in, and Martin and Monica followed along by sight.

Brightly beams our Father's mercy
From his lighthouse ever more,

52

But to us he gives the keeping
Of the lights along the shore.

With the chorus Monica realized that a bass rumble
had been added from Mr. Brice's corner.

Let the lower lights be burning,
Send a gleam across the wave;
And some struggling, fainting seaman
You may rescue, you may save.

They went on through the hymnbook, everyone singing, and then onto old songs, sentimental ones, that made
Monica homesick for she didn't know what. This is like
something in a book, she thought. Like the stories about
Old Times that I always loved because they sounded so
cozy and so safe.

They finished off the evening with cookies and milk
around the kitchen table. Mellowed by the music, Mr.
Brice was practically genial, and told Martin to come in
any time he felt like pumping a tune out of the old organ.
Good nights were said in a sort of mutual glow.

Homer and the dogs walked home with them. The
fog had gone, the sky was crowded with stars; the Milky
Way was a broad luminous road from horizon to horizon.
It was a very quiet night with no surf on the shore. Distantly they could hear a bell-buoy clanging.

"We could be on the top of a mountain," said Monica.
"We're approaching a fantastic castle built on a peak by
a mad king."

"A mad Sanborn, you mean," said Martin. They

53

flashed their lights over windows and porches and gables. Homer pointed his powerful five-cell torch up at an attic window tucked tightly under the eaves.

"What would you do if you saw a light up there?" he asked.

"I'd think the Monster was reading late," said Monica.

"Is that the locked room?" asked Martin. His words fell oddly into the night silence. "Well, *is* it?" he insisted.

"What locked room?" Homer asked.

"There's one up there in the attic," Monica said. "You must know about it. Anyway, Martin's dying of curiosity."

"I guess I know now what one you mean." Homer yawned. "Heck, I never thought about it one way or the other."

"You mean to say you've been all over that house and you've never been in that room?" Martin asked.

"That's what I mean to say. Gramp doesn't have the keys, and I figger it's a sore spot with him, like they don't trust him or something. Anyway, I asked him about it once and he got mad as a wet hen, so if you want to stay on the good side of him don't *you* mention it."

"He won't," Monica assured him. "Martin, you kill off your insatiable curiosity once and for all, at least about that room."

He grunted something, and once they were inside with a lamp lit he said, "Let's go up and see if that window *is* in the locked room. I think we could tell by looking out of another one."

54

"Chummy, you sound mighty confused to me," Homer told him, "and besides, you won't catch me up in that attic at night. I'm a coward and I don't mind admitting it. The hair's standing up on the back of my neck right now. Hey, can I borrow a book?" he asked Monica. "It's all right, I've borrowed books before out of this house and always brought them back. This morning I was trying to remember something out of *Twenty Thousand Leagues Under the Sea*, so I'd kind of like to read it again."

In the living room the boys searched for the book. Monica watched them in the soft circle of lamplight, one slim and dark, one compact and blond, each attractive in his own fashion. Their faces were lively and expressive as they discussed the books they were handling. Homer had read a good many, it turned out . . . Sleepy, relaxed, Monica wondered about Homer. She'd known other boys and sometimes had been friends with one; they'd gone riding bicycles together, exploring whatever city or region they were in, visiting cathedrals and museums and old palaces. But to be this informal with a boy was new to her, and Homer himself was strange enough to her to border on the exotic. There'd never be any long, involved, exciting arguments with Homer about Life, but then that sort of thing didn't belong here. Homer did belong. He seemed exactly right for his world.

Seemed. That was the key word. Because they didn't really know Homer yet. He was capable and friendly, he liked fast engines, he could tease and be teased, his eyes were very blue and his smile contagious. But beyond that—

Be careful, Monica, she warned herself coldly. Be very careful. Yes, I know this place calls for a love affair, but the idylls exist only in poems and paintings.

With a small shock she realized that Homer was watching her. Squatting on his heels before the shelves, he was looking over his shoulder at her. "Now here's something just right for you," Martin was running on. "A complete set of *The Bobbsey Twins*. Really blood-curdling stuff."

Homer and Monica regarded each other steadily. And then, just when it seemed that one or the other must say something, a dog barked from far off in the house. Homer sprang to his feet. "I clean forgot those critters!" He ran out into the hall, whistling.

"They're all right," Martin called after him. "They smell the Monster, that's all!"

Homer returned with two panting, wriggling dogs. But Babe kept looking back over her shoulder. Homer told her crossly to lie down and she did, but lay with her chin on her paws, facing away from the lamplight and toward the door with watchful eyes. George put his head in Monica's lap and she ran her hands through his thick mane, murmuring to him.

"There's something in behind Old Jules Verne," Martin said. "A box, by the feel. Wooden, carved. Somebody's summer handcraft, and they couldn't stand to look at it afterward so they hid it." He pulled out more books, and then brought out a small chest of dark pol-

ished wood whose lid carried a narrow border of exqui-
sitely detailed carving.

"That's nobody's occupational therapy," said Monica.
"It's a work of art.   Can it be opened?"

Martin tried the small latch.   "Here's my knife," said
Homer eagerly, but Martin shook his head.

"I wouldn't want to force it.   It might mar the finish."

"Then how in Tophet can you find out what's in it?"

Suddenly the lid sprang open, and they looked upon a
set of tiny silver figures.   Somebody drew a sharp, hissing
breath; it could have been any one of them.

"Look," Martin whispered.   "Henry the Eighth."   He
picked up the minute and perfect monarch.

"And Francis the First."   Monica's own voice was
hushed as she touched the other king.   "Martin, it's the
set they call 'The Field of the Cloth of Gold.'   Remember seeing one like it in that museum?"

Homer's square-tipped fingers fondled with curious
delicacy an armed knight, a little queen, then darted to
an ornate castle.   "What are they?   Just to look at?"

"It's a chess set, not that we'd know if we hadn't already seen one like it," Monica said.   "Do you ever play
chess?"

"I haven't got the brains for it," said Homer candidly.
"Gramp plays Gumpy, and there's a chess club over to
the Port.   But I'll bet none of them ever saw anything
like this before."   He leaned close over the figures, which
seemed to gleam with their own soft radiance.   "How
come I didn't know it was here?   I thought I knew just
about everything there was in this house."

57

"Except for the locked room," said Martin. Homer ignored that.

"You sure you fellers didn't bring this with you?"

"We didn't," said Martin.

"When you're picking out books," said Monica, "you aren't likely to go groping in behind them unless you suspect there's something there. So it was easy for you to overlook."

"Then for Pete's sake why'd *you* start poking around?" He scowled at Martin.

"Because I have a suspicious nature. I always poke around in bookcases in hope of finding a million dollars in old bills hidden away by an eccentric ancestor."

"Well, I think this must be worth something," said Monica. "Not a million dollars, of course, but *something*. But not to us."

"Why not?" demanded Homer. His blue eyes were intense. "You're Sanborns, aren't you? The stuff's here, nobody's using it—"

Disturbed, Monica shut down the lid. "I think it had better go back where Martin found it." She wanted to add, *I wish he hadn't found it,* but that was silly, there was no reason for this sudden discomfort. "It's probably the personal property of one of the family," she went on, "and if he's dead he must have heirs."

"I'm going to take it up to my tower and play myself a game of chess" Martin said.

"Martin, please put it back behind the books," she said quietly. She saw the resistance in him, the argument rising in his eyes and coming to his lips, and repeated her request in the same quiet but final tone. It was not often she used it, and she was always surprised and relieved when Martin obeyed. He did now, his lower lip expressing annoyance. Homer picked up his book.

"Well, I'm shoving off," he said curtly.

"See you tomorrow?" Martin cheered up. "I want to take you sailing and scare you to death."

"You aren't getting the chance, chummy. I'll take you two out for a real ride, slapping through those crests with the water flying, but it won't be tomorrow because I got to go ashore with Gramp."

"Don't forget supper," Monica warned him.

"No, ma'am. I'm expecting some of that fancy French cooking."

They went out into the overgrown garden, fragrant with roses in the starlight. The dogs coursed down toward the beach. "Looking for ghost rabbits," said Martin.

"Ayuh, we'd ought to stock the place just for them," said Homer. "Well, sleep tight and don't let the ghosties bite."

They all laughed, and he whistled to the dogs and set off toward the woods. The dog-whistle turned into a gay tune that rang out sweetly in the stillness, and Monica's pleasure returned as sharply and suddenly as it had left.

7

T HE GHOSTIES neither bit nor walked, as far as the two knew. They slept deeply and woke to a clear morning and the prospect of having the island completely to themselves for a whole day. "You're sure you don't want to go to the mainland with the Brices?" Monica asked Martin.

"I don't want to change our luck. Once we step foot on the mainland we're likely to bring something crashing down on our heads."

"Evil forces," she said with wry humor. "But they can't touch us here." She looked around at a blue and golden world, breathed honeysuckle and salt water, heard a thrush and then a gull, and went to work contentedly on a grocery list. Mrs. Brice had said she'd shop for them.

Martin sat on the porch railing, whittling and whistling. He was barefoot, wearing old shorts, and already turned to a gypsy brown. Yes, it was true that nothing could touch them here. Even time seemed to stand still.

Martin suggested rowing the dory around to Brices' cove with the list, and then exploring among the islands while the water held its morning calm. Monica put a lunch together and they started out. When they left the list with Mr. Brice, who was at the wharf, his stern gaunt face did not seem so forbidding, and he even called after them, "Have a good time, but take care you don't drown yourselves."

"He's nice," Monica said contentedly. "So is Mrs. Brice."

"Homer's all right too. Let's go straight for that little island there, with the old stone wall on it. It's called Nubbin."

"Let me try rowing then." They changed places and Monica wrestled with the oars, which seemed to be animated by a life of their own. Martin's comments were no help and the sun was hot, and the little island didn't seem to come any closer. But quite a few blisters later, after a good deal of frustration, she achieved the proper rhythm, and knew the ineffable thrill of feeling the dory glide forward over the water at her command.

Exploring Nubbin took only a short time and they went on to the next. Each had its own enchantment, if only a display of wild flowers, an ancient wall, a family of eider ducks in a cove. Off one island they fished for pollock which flashed under the boat as if through liquid emerald, swarming for the hooks baited with periwinkles. Having no way to keep fish during a long warm day in the dory, they threw them back as fast they caught them, but Monica intended to catch some on purpose one day to try in a trout recipe she'd learned in France.

Leaving this spot, they came around a long rocky point to discover Gumpy hauling lobster traps, so they stopped to watch this process from start to finish. "You picked any field strawberries yet?" he asked Monica. "You go

61

right ashore on Garnet and get ye a dish out of my camp, and you can pick yourself a quart in no time."

"I'd love to," she said. "Shall we pick you a dish too?"

His leathery face creased in a wide grin. "Well, now, Missy, I was hoping you'd get the idea. I can't bend down so good as I used to."

"There'll be a big bowl of strawberries waiting for you."

"You want to go deep-sea fishing with me tomorrow, boy?" he asked Martin.

"Yes, *sir!*"

"I'll pick you up in the morning 'bout five-thutty. You row out to your mooring there in the cove."

"Yes, *sir!*" Martin said again, his grin blazing.

He was not nearly so enthusiastic about picking wild strawberries, and went off exploring Garnet. Monica didn't care. She had picked field strawberries before in her life, but never on a treeless hump of rock and turf set between so much sky and sea that the island seemed to be a star adrift in clear blue space. Gumpy's two tiger cats helped her search through the tall grass for the sprays of plump deep red berries. She had two quarts almost too soon, left one of them in the small tidy cabin, and bid the cats an affectionate farewell.

They talked about owning islands while they rowed leisurely back to Sea Island. Ducks dived at their approach and then came up again to watch them, paddling gulls were too sophisticated to fly away. As they approached Sea Island under the high western end, Monica watching for the first glimpse of the beach below the house, they heard a powerful outboard, and then a white speedboat with a broad windshield roared into sight ahead of them, seemed to point straight at them like a deadly missile, then swerved sharply off to disappear between Nubbin and Kestrel.

Martin rested his oars and stared over his shoulder at the foaming wake. "Did he just come away from the island?"

"Sounds deceive you around the water. He might have been cruising along close to shore just looking at the place and all the signs, and the point cut off the sound of the engine. Anyway, the dogs stay down at the shore when the Brices are away."

"By now most of the local people must know those two dogs couldn't back up those signs." He laughed. "Babe was wagging her tail at a mouse yesterday because it sat up and squeaked at her. She all but apologized out loud."

"But this might be what Homer calls a summer complaint. For all he knows, there could be a pack of wolves out here."

The wolves met them at the beach, accompanied them to the house.

Martin ran ahead leaping from ledge to ledge like a young deer, the dogs racing around him. I feel about twelve years old, Monica thought, like that time when we lived in Rome and we were all so happy and it seemed as if it would go on forever and there'd never again be anything to worry about ...

Suddenly the dogs burst into a frenzy of barking and

she almost crashed into Martin's back as he stopped short. At the head of the wide front steps a man stood watching them. He was slight, wearing dark-rimmed glasses, and his graying dark hair fell over his forehead. He gave them a wide, charming smile and said gently, "Hello, children. I'm your Uncle Theo."

The earth seemed to rock under Monica's feet, the house shimmered against the sky. "How do you do, sir?" Martin's most formal voice said. Everything steadied. She slid a glance at her brother and saw sweat on his forehead, a familiar tightness around his mouth, but nobody else would know what that meant. He advanced to shake hands as if this surprise were really a pleasant one. "Be quiet," he said to the dogs, who obeyed.

Beaming, Uncle Theo clasped Martin's hand and reached out with his left one for Monica's. "This is— er—wonderful, you know! Simply wonderful." Of course that loving-kindness wasn't true. He was just preparing for the kill. Numbly she put her hand in his and felt it warmly squeezed.

"When the Brices told me Tom's children were here I could hardly believe my—er—ears! I was very close to Tom, you know. Very close. But alas, circumstances— er—thrust us a world apart. We lost touch, literally. Tragic." He blinked, and then smiled again. "Unfortunately I never met your dear mother. Madam and I—er —had come to a contretemps about *my* marriage before— er—Lydia's arrival on the scene. But your father wrote me about their—er—elopement, and I sent them my blessing, for what it was worth. We must have some—er—good talks about your dear father."

He released their hands, then seemed troubled. "You children are very tense. Perhaps you feel that old Uncle Theo's arrival is—er—inopportune?"

Somewhere during the last few moments Monica had found herself. "We're afraid of you," she said honestly. "You see, we're here without permission, but the Brices don't know that. We were brought up on stories of Sea House, and when we came back to this country we thought we might never get a chance to see it unless we made it, so we ran away."

Uncle Theo nodded at intervals, absently patting the nearest dog. When she finished he broke into soft laughter. "But I'm here without permission, too! I've run away also, in a manner of speaking. So our mutual guilt should be our—er—mutual protection, don't you agree?"

"Yes, sir, we do," said Martin strongly.

"But you're an adult," Monica pointed out. "You can do what you want."

He chuckled. "There's a difference of opinion on that point. If Madam were alive today even my gray hairs wouldn't—er—convince her, and I'm afraid Alonzo Ferris feels the same way. Of course he was *born* ancient. I don't believe any one of that firm ever had a young impulse in his life."

"Are they the ones you're running away from?" Monica asked.

He nodded. "They're frightfully stuffy about—er—

65

members of the family coming here on their own. Presumably we'll load our luggage with all the—er—loot we can carry and abscond with it."

"But in the meantime nobody uses the place," argued Martin. "How long is it going to be left like this?"

Uncle Theo shrugged like a Parisian. "Your great-grandmother refused to listen to whole regiments of lawyers, and left the property loaded with—er—hopeless complications. By now there are about two dozen heirs scattered over the world, at least two-thirds of whom care nothing about the place, and the—er—remaining third must lurk, sneak, prowl like—er—thieves in the night, even to lay eyes on the place."

He turned bleak and older before their eyes. Then the twinkling smile came back. "Well, now, I've come lurking, sneaking, prowling back to feast my eyes on re-membered treasures that Madam was too angry to take with her when she closed up the place. Otherwise, I'd never have gotten to see them again in this life. As for meals," he added briskly, "I daresay I can board with the Brices. I don't intend to complicate your adventure."

Suddenly moved, Monica said swiftly, "Please have your meals with us, Uncle Theo. And I'll make your bed now, if you tell me where your room is."

"You're so kind." He blinked hard. "Thank you."

"Then I'll do something about supper. We're supposed to have company too, Homer Brice."

"Oh, is he the grandson? He didn't come back with us. His grandparents were quite concerned because they'd lost track of him."

66

"He may appear yet," said Monica. "You two had better go home," she said to the dogs. "Your father and mother are back."

As if they understood, the dogs went pounding off past the rose thickets. "Now I'll begin my sentimental journey," said Uncle Theo. They heard him singing under his breath in the living room as they went upstairs to change. Martin stopped at Monica's door.

"Talk about comrades in crime," he whispered. *"And* blackmail. *And* collusion. And . . . . He may not be a Sanborn at all. We've heard Father mention Tom's Uncle Theo, but how do we know he's *it?"*

"Maybe he isn't. Maybe he's a leprechaun. In fact I'm—er—sure of it."

They doubled up in weak, witless laughter.

8

UNCLE THEO's authenticity was proved, at least to Monica, by his appearance in many photographs in her room. To Martin she pointed out a boyish Theo surrounded happily by girls in the playclothes of forty years ago.

"That doesn't prove he's a Sanborn," Martin was stubborn. "He could have been visiting."

"But here he is again, with Madam. Look! The same eyes, the same cant to the head."

"Well, maybe," Martin grumbled. "Whoever he is, I wish he hadn't picked out this time to run away."

"I wish it too, but it could have been worse." How, she didn't know, and was glad Martin didn't challenge her. They were in her room after supper, while she put on fresh lipstick before going to the Brices' to collect their grocery order. The meal had been a light one, finished off with the strawberries. Homer hadn't appeared. Uncle Theo, after gracefully praising the food, had gone wandering through the house searching for remembered treasures.

Martin stood disconsolately by the window, and Monica said, "Didn't you like hearing about the time they landed on Nubbin to look for buried treasure, and the dory went adrift, and Father swam after it? The trouble was, I wanted to shout 'That was my father!' "

"It mixes everything up." His face was strained.

"We're neither one thing nor the other. With the Brices it was easy, because we knew more about the Sanborns than they did. But he *is* a Sanborn. I keep thinking I'll put my foot in it."

"I do too," she admitted. "But on the other hand I'm going to find out from him all I can about Father . . . as long as I remember to call him Mark Christie."

"This was going to be our time and nobody else's," he gloomed. "Nobody was going to be blowing down our necks."

She couldn't dwell on it or let him do so. As they left the room they heard from down the hall a tinkling little piano tune, and a light, pleasant tenor voice. " 'Believe me if all those endearing young charms—' "

Martin growled, "Blessings on thee, little man, why'd you have to have this plan?" Monica laughed, and he couldn't help joining her. They went out in a better mood, and he offered to transport her to the Brices' in the Sea Island Mercedes, or wheelbarrow.

"Well!" Mrs. Brice greeted them. "Weren't you surprised to see your uncle?"

"It was a double surprise," said Monica, "because we'd never seen him before."

Mrs. Brice laughed merrily. "He was some flabbergasted when he heard you two were here!"

"I'll bet," said Martin. "We've signed a nonaggression pact. He won't watch us and we won't watch him."

Even Mr. Brice smiled slightly at that, then grew even more amiable and said, "Give us a tune on the organ before you go back, boy."

While Martin played, Monica sat on the doorstep with Mrs. Brice. The old-fashioned music brought her a throat-clutching loneliness for her parents. She felt lost, adrift, as if she would be a stranger wherever she went. For a little while she and Martin had fooled themselves into thinking they belonged here, but Uncle Theo had put an end to that.

"I don't know what became of Homer today," Mrs. Brice was saying, and Monica eagerly turned her attention to that.

"We'd asked him to supper," she said.

"He told me that this morning. And then he went off while we was over to Port George and never come back. My friend told me she saw him in that Pooch Robey's car in the afternoon, heading for Limerock. *That Pooch.*" She sounded worried and disapproving. "Nice car, nice boat, and as far as I can see he never does a hand's turn of work from one month to the next."

Monica's thoughts drifted among the glimmer of Queen Anne's Lace in the fields, and the shine of light surf along the shore. If Homer had been here she'd have asked him to go for a walk. This hushed hour was meant for walking. It could be casual and friendly. *Oh, I'm dying for a walk, Homer, but I don't want to go alone. Come on.* And then if he didn't know enough to take her hand, or kiss her under a spruce tree, she'd know once and for all that intent look the other night didn't mean a thing.

She shrugged, and Mrs. Brice said, "Midges getting you? No-see-ems, the Indians called the pesky things, and that's a good name. Let's go in."

70

The organ had stopped, and Martin and Mr. Brice were talking. "Yep, they had the sheriff down to look things over," Mr. Brice was saying. "He came in town today and was asking questions about the boys. No chance of Homer being in on it, he's been right here last three or four nights."

"Of course Homer wouldn't be in on it!" Mrs. Brice broke in. "Whether he was here or not! The way you talk, Elmore!"

"In on what?" Monica asked.

"Breaking into summer places over on the mainland," Martin explained. "There's been a lot of it going on."

"I guess there's no call to worry about Sea House," said Mr. Brice. "Nobody dares to land on the island that's got no business to."

"Not with the dogs," said Mrs. Brice complacently.

Martin gave a skeptical glance at the bright eyes and always-ready-to-wag tails, but said nothing.

When they got home, accompanied by the dogs, a small lamp burned in the kitchen, but there was neither sight nor sound of Uncle Theo. "I suppose he's all tucked in with his Teddy bear," said Martin. "That one up in the playroom was probably his till he left home." Monica, putting away the things he handed to her from the grocery box, didn't answer, and he shrugged. "Oh, all right. He seems like a harmless old bird, and maybe we can stay out of each other's hair."

Martin got up before five, packed his own lunch, and was gone with Gumpy when Monica got up. Uncle Theo had also arisen, fixed his breakfast, and disappeared. She took a tray out to the front steps for her fa-

71

vorite morning view. What would she do today? Wash some underwear and socks. Swim again. Beachcomb for bits of twisty driftwood and seaworn scraps of glass turned amethyst by the sun. Perhaps find an arrowhead. Take a book to read by the water or in some birchy glade. Perhaps she could leave lunch ready for Uncle Theo and take her own with her.

As she carried her tray in, she heard his little tune from the dining room, and went in to ask him about lunch. He held out the cup in his hand. It belonged to the green and white set in the cabinet.

"Isn't this exquisite? I've seen these lovely things in my dreams for years, and to find them all here, intact, just as I last saw them, is to turn the clock back and make me a youth again."

"It *is* beautiful china."

"*Porcelain,* my dear! Oriental Lowestoft, dating from about 1820." She noticed that now he didn't use the nervous little "er"; he must have been really thrown off balance yesterday, because of her and Martin's unexpected presence. Today he was more at home, and carried on by excitement. "It's not really Lowestoft, you know. It's Chinese porcelain, but somebody once gave Lowestoft credit for this marvelous ware, and the label stuck even after the truth was known. It's very valuable. Madam must have been in a terrible temper when she left, to leave this all behind."

"The house is full of lovely things," Monica said. "This part of the coast must be the most honest place in the world."

"I'm sure of that," he said solemnly. "And this is the most wonderful porcelain. Priceless. Well, not literally. A complete set of this particular pattern brought $18,000 at an auction last year."

All that money sitting here for years, Monica thought bitterly, and if my brother and I had that much in the bank—But *no*, at fifteen and seventeen we're still supposed to be too young to manage ourselves. She forced down the familiar rebellion and tried to listen to Uncle Theo.

"Have you come across my sister's—your Aunt Peggy's Royal Doulton figurines yet?" he asked. "Perhaps she took them with her to California. And another thing is my chess set. Father gave it to me before he died, if I can ever prove it to our grim trustees." He replaced the cup in the cupboard, and caressed a large tureen. "Many dishes of lobster stew have been served from that." He sighed, looking older again, and Monica wanted to cheer him.

"What sort of chess set is it?" she asked.

"It's called 'The Field of the Cloth of Gold.' It represents Henry the Eighth and Francis the First and their respective courts at their great meeting, you know. I have dearly loved that set since I was first allowed to handle the pieces," he said wistfully.

"Oh, we've—" Monica stopped short, then finished, "We've seen a set like that in England." Something about him made her feel motherly, and she wanted to surprise him by having the carved chest appear magically before him.

73

"Madam may have given it away in a moment of caprice," he said. "She did have such moments. Quite terrifying in their own way . . . I think I shall ask Mrs. Brice if she's come across any of these things in her cleaning. I have a little list." He waved it at Monica and went out before she could find out about lunch.

She ran to the living room and pulled out the set of Jules Verne. Her fingers groped in dusty space and at last brushed the back wall of the deep shelf. At first she thought she'd guessed the location wrong, and pulled out more books to the left and the right, until daylight streamed in upon the shelf and revealed nothing but a few thin books lying on their sides and some magazines from twenty or more years ago. Clear in the thin film of dust was the shape of the absent box.

Martin must have disobeyed her and taken the set to his room after all. She went up to the tower, but there was no sign of the set here. She looked in all the bureau drawers and in the closet. Now the first seedling of alarm began to sprout. She lost all desire to beachcomb, swim, or read; she could think only of how far away Martin was, somewhere ten or twelve miles outside the islands with Gumpy, happily catching big codfish.

She glanced into some of the other rooms but she knew the search was futile. Unable to face making conversation with Uncle Theo, she fixed a salad and a sandwich for him, left them in the refrigerator, and set a tray for him with a note on it. Then she went out, taking a sandwich she was sure she couldn't eat, and a book she wouldn't read. There was a high sunny ledge in the woods where one could look through spruce tops out to sea, and she settled there, wondering if she could will Martin ashore by concentration.

"There's nothing to be so frightened about," she reasoned aloud. "Nobody's going to accuse you and Martin of stealing anything, because nobody knows the box was behind the books except Martin and me, and—*Homer*."

It was like a punch in the stomach. But it can't be Homer! she cried in silence. It couldn't *possibly* be! He's not that kind. Why, his grandfather's the caretaker. Homer wouldn't do anything like that, no matter how much he was tempted.

"Martin, for heaven's sake please come home," she wailed softly. "So I can find out for sure that you put that chest away in another place for perfectly logical reasons."

9

SHE WAS EATING her sandwich with desperation rather than hunger when she heard a blessedly familiar engine. She ran down through the spruces, across the hot meadow behind the house and the rocky one before it, and was panting on the sand by the time Martin was climbing from Gumpy's boat into the anchored dory. Gumpy handed him his lunch box and a very large codfish. He waved both arms at Monica and shouted, "I brought back most of him!"

He pointed *Miss Alice* out of the cove in the direction of the Brices' landing, evidently to take them some fish. Martin rowed quickly ashore, got out before the dory was properly beached, and splashed sea water over his face and hair. "I was seasick," he groaned. *"Was* I seasick! Why I ever thought deep-sea fishing was one version of Paradise—"

"You thought so because Father brought you up so."

"But he never told me about lying there rocking in those deep swells that come rolling all the way from Spain, and the hot sun drawing out all those unforgettable odors of last year's bait—" His voice trailed off and he grew even paler. "Gumpy told me it was no disgrace, but that didn't improve the situation." He gazed with intense distaste at the fish on the dory seat. It had been gutted, but still retained its head and seemed to gaze back at Martin with the same disgust. "Can you do anything

76

with *that?* I caught plenty, by the way, before I was overcome. Gumpy's going to salt and dry them."

"I can do a lot of things with a nice fresh codfish. Poach, bake, broil, fry——"

"Spare me," said Martin, "and heave-ho on the dory." They hauled her up on the sand and made her fast, and Martin collapsed with a groan. "Dear Terra Firma, dear land of our fathers, dear——"

"Martin," his sister said. "Did you move the chess set from the bookshelf to some other place?"

"What chess set? Oh!" He sat up briskly. "What's wrong?"

"It's not there." Already she knew that Martin hadn't touched it. She told him quickly what had happened, and waited for the shock to hit.

"But only you and I and Homer," he began. *"No.* It can't be Homer."

"It can't be either of us. So who else could it be?"

"Listen, we're taking it for granted that nobody else in the world knows that chess set was hidden there. What if somebody was looking in the window when we discovered it that night? Remember how the dogs acted?"

"They were upstairs barking, I know."

"Sure! Somebody could even have been in the house, so they heard a suspicious sound. But Homer made them come and stay with us, so the somebody could have sneaked out by whatever way he sneaked in, and then could have been looking in the windows."

"And when we went outside the dogs were chasing all around, and Babe ran down to the shore," said Monica

77

happily. "After ghost rabbits, you said." It was a relief not to suspect Homer. Of course she wanted Uncle Theo to have his chess set, but to discover that a friend was a thief was a worse tragedy than the loss of the set.

"That speedboat we saw yesterday when we were coming home," she said. "That man could actually have been on the island after all, and taken the chess set and heaven knows what else. You said yourself that there must be somebody else who knows the dogs aren't really vicious. Gumpy could have mentioned it to someone without thinking, or Homer could have. It might even be someone he brought out here sometime."

"Wait a minute! How do we know that dear pixilated Uncle Leprechaun Theo hasn't already lifted the chess set? Maybe all this searching is just a smoke screen. He'll leave for his hollow tree being very sad about the whole thing, and sell it as fast he can."

"I don't believe that," said Monica flatly. "I think Uncle Theo is just what he says he is. And he really liked Father, don't forget. I'm for Uncle Theo because of that, if for nothing else."

Martin shrugged. "What'll we do, tell Homer? He'd know about everybody around here, he might have some ideas— No, wait a minute!" The light of adventure blazed in his face. "Let's not tell *anybody* yet. Let's see if the character comes back. I'd like to catch him in the act. And he may even be the one who's breaking into those summer places."

There were times when she was the sure-footed one, quieting her brother's doubts, moving serenely ahead. But when it came to intrigue Martin was the master.

He loved espionage stories, and had no doubts of his own probable success as a secret agent. Still, as the oldest, she was bound to point out certain facts.

"In the meantime the chess set can disappear for good."

"It could be gone already, if your idea about that speedboat is right. No, I'll bet you anything he'll be back. He knows how to get into the house and he's not afraid of the dogs. He could land anywhere in calm weather, he wouldn't need a beach."

"But we're responsible," Monica protested. "We're living here in the house, and he mightn't have found out about the chess set, ever, if you hadn't found it. If we think it's stolen we ought to tell somebody."

"And be suspected *ourselves?*"

They stood facing each other, olive cheeks flushed, their dark eyes brilliant. "Oh *blast,*" Martin hissed. "Here comes Peter Pan. Listen, if we haven't caught the fella by the time Aunt Naomi's forces begin to close in on us, we'll tell. How's that?"

Not very good, but she had no time to argue, even if she could think of arguments, because Uncle Theo was too close. They put on the proper faces as he joined them.

"What a magnificent fish!" he remarked. "Did you get him out on the Frying Pan Shoal?"

"Do you know about that, sir?" Martin was respectfully surprised.

"Many's the prime codfish I've pulled over the gunnel out on the Frying Pan Shoal. Many's the breakfast I lost, too."

Martin grinned. "Then I guess I really joined the club today."

Over a supper of golden-brown cod steaks, Uncle Theo said sadly that neither Brice remembered ever seeing the chess set. "Not that Mrs. Brice goes around poking her nose into other folks' affairs, she'll have you know, so she wouldn't have opened the box if she'd seen it. But she can't remember seeing it. So—" He shrugged. "My only hope is that whoever has it cherishes it."

Uncomfortably they agreed with him, and then Martin was inspired to tell about seeing a family of porpoises this morning, which led Uncle Theo into memoirs of his experience as a boy, trying to tame a porpoise. The chess set wasn't brought up again.

Uncle Theo retired right after supper to write letters and read in bed. Martin and Monica took a walk around the wildest rockiest part of the shore, piling up driftwood with hopeful thoughts of beach picnics and bonfires. Enjoying herself, Monica wished the thief would return tonight, while she was still in this mood of airy confidence and everything seemed possible.

When they came back to the home beach, Homer was there. They greeted him with enthusiasm made even warmer by the fact that they'd briefly suspected him, and he seemed pleased to receive such a welcome. He'd brought them a bag of peaches.

"How did you know I liked peaches better than any other fruit in the world?" Monica teased him.

He said, deadpan, "I've got second sight, and when I saw that basket of peaches your face was printed on every one of them."

"If I can break in on this intimate conversation," said Martin, "what happened to you last night?"

"Last night?" He blinked and scowled. "Oh, yeah. Gorry, I'm sorry I didn't get to have supper with you, but something came up and I didn't have a chance even to tell Grammy. I guess I ought to tell you now that it's likely to happen again. If I get a chance at a job, even if it's only for a day, I grab it."

"That's all right," Monica assured him. "We'll understand."

He was very earnest. "This was worth a ten-spot to me. I went to Limerock and drove back a summer gink's car for him. He'd had it overhauled at the Cadillac place up there. Gorry, by the time I got back to the Port with that Caddy I felt like I ought to pay him for the privilege." He whistled.

"Some day I'm going to have a Rolls," said Martin. "Let's go up and get something to eat."

"How about some music on the old piano?" Homer asked. "I bet you can make that thing talk."

"The trouble is, nobody offers me any ten-spots for that."

In the kitchen they ate crackers and cheese and peaches, and then went upstairs to the ballroom. Monica hushed the boys, who were being elaborately foolish, and tiptoed to Uncle Theo's door. When she heard him humming, she knocked softly. "We're going to play the piano. Will it disturb you?"

"Bless you, child, no. I'll enjoy it. I'll dream on the days gone by."

"Uncle Theo, you're not that old," she said severely,

81

and he laughed. He did rather overdo being the lovable old codger, and that laugh proved that he knew it.

Martin began by playing the old popular songs their father had taught him, and they all sang. Then Homer asked Monica to dance, but neither knew the modern dances that the other did, and the project looked like a failure until Martin swung into a waltz. Homer was a smooth and substantial partner, and it was a pleasure to dance with him. As they glided away from the lamplight into the dusk, they moved together as if in a shared dream of effortless motion. Homer always looked and smelled freshly scrubbed, his skin was clear and healthy, his arm was strong around her. How much do I like him? she asked herself. I was sick to think he took the chess set, but I'd feel that way about any friend. If he kissed me, then I would know . . . She wished he would, but the wishing was calm, like this mood that possessed them, like drifting on a windless twilight sea.

They were at the far end of the long room now, and the polished floor glimmered in the dusk like an actual sea. Now was the time for Homer to kiss her, and he was leaning his cheek against hers and holding her a little closer. It was very nice. She liked it. But why don't you kiss me? she asked him in silence. Suddenly he tightened his arm even more and stopped short, and in the gloom they stared at each other, their faces drawing nearer to one another.

Then at the other end of the room Martin crashed into "The Stars and Stripes Forever".

Homer and Monica jumped as if firecrackers had exploded under their feet. "Boy, *he's* a help!" Homer muttered. Roughly he pulled her arm through his and marched her back to the piano. Monica was angry with Martin for choosing that moment to be whimsical. Or had he suspected something, guessed that they weren't moving in those distant shadows? But in the lamplight he appeared innocently absorbed as he thumped away with great fervor. She would never know even if she asked him, and to ask him would be to give herself away.

All at once her face burned. Wanting a boy to kiss her so she could tell if she liked him or not! She was acting like the worst kind of nitwit! What would Father think? Depression swamped her. She wanted to get away to her room—no, not *her* room, she had no room here or anywhere, she didn't belong. But at least she could lock a door, and behind it she could cry and cry, and wish they'd never done such a wrong and crazy thing as coming to Sea House.

Homer seemed to have gotten rapidly over his disappointment. He and Martin were back to laughing at each other's inane jokes. They returned to the kitchen for more food, and were so oblivious of Monica's mood that she felt more and more lonesome. Then while Martin was trying to work out a silly match trick Homer had shown him, Homer winked at her past Martin's ear; his eyes were as sunny and blue as the cove at noon, and at once everything fell back into place. There'd be another chance, if they wanted it badly enough, and it had been really funny, after all.

10

THEY WENT part way home with him, and were invited to have a ride the next day in *The Blue Streak*. After they'd left him and were walking back, Martin said, "I wonder if anybody will try anything tonight."

"Earlier I was wishing he would, but now I hope he needs sleep as much as I do." She yawned enormously. There was a rush of feet behind them, a loud panting and snorting, and the dogs arrived.

"I've got the idea of the century," said Martin. "We'll let George and Babe do the work tonight." He dropped his voice to a conspirator's whisper. "We'll keep them in the house. If they're outside and they meet the crook, they won't make a fuss because he's made friends with them. But inside they'll be on the alert for any strange noise, and they'll wake us. Of course I don't intend to sleep too hard," he added. "A good secret agent sleeps with one ear and one eye open."

"I'll have to come in and see that phenomenon," said Monica on another yawn. Invited in, the dogs pushed past them through the woodshed and threw themselves down on the kitchen floor. Uncle Theo had left a lamp burning.

"Yessir, we've got the right idea," Martin exulted.

"But when we hear somebody, then what?" Monica asked. "How do we corner him?"

"There's a .22 pistol put away in a box in the back of my closet." His eyes were darkly shining in the lamp-light. "It was all wrapped up and clean, but I've cleaned it again."

"Oh, *Martin!*" She shut off her exclamation of dis-may, and said coldly, "Well, you can just pretend you never found it."

"For Pete's sake, it's not loaded and I haven't any shells for it," he said in disgust. "But it *looks* deadly, and that's enough."

"It's too much. What if he's got a loaded gun, and he thinks you're going to use yours, so he shoots? You aren't going to wave any pistol around. No, no, *no*." At this George and Babe went behind the stove.

"What else are we supposed to do?" He struck a pose, hands on hips. "Say, you crook, you, we've got you dead to rights and you can just put down whatever you're car-rying there, and we want Uncle Theo's chess set back *too*. Right now, or I'll kick you in the shins."

Monica collapsed giggling into a chair, and the dogs rushed out to her, sure that the crisis was over. Martin glared at them all. "Oh, I don't know," Monica said. "Maybe I'm too sleepy to think straight, but just getting a good look at him should be enough. Then we could describe him to other people, who would recognize him."

Martin still looked adamant, and she said, "Promise me you won't bring out the gun." This tone used to work when Martin was four. He was fifteen now, and it didn't work.

85

"I'll promise nothing of the sort," he said with dignity. "I'll act as the spirit moves me. Now let's go to bed."

They agreed each to take a dog, but to leave their doors open so the dogs could move around if they wanted to. The dogs were wildly enthusiastic about the new project, and the more they were shushed on the stairs the more they panted and whined, while toenails rattled in crescendoes of joy. There was no light showing under Uncle Theo's door, and the dogs sniffed so loudly at the crack that Monica wanted to burst into silly giggles again. If Uncle Theo believed in ghosts he'd be lying there with chattering teeth thinking phantom wolves were after him.

When she woke up it was sunrise, and Babe was sprawled across the foot of the bed in deep sleep. The house could have been stolen out from under us for all we'd have known, Monica thought. Babe rolled over and arched her back and waved her feet in the air, and laughed at Monica upside down; Monica laughed back. Joining Martin and George downstairs, she was relieved to know that they'd heard nothing.

They let the dogs out, cautioning them not to tell where they'd spent the night, and the dogs streaked toward home and the warm breakfast they always had after their night duty. Uncle Theo came down humming "All Things Bright and Beautiful", and said, "Ah, who could ask for more than to be surrounded by fresh young faces at breakfast? And last night I dreamed my chess set was in the attic, so I'm going to search there today."

86

"Do you know anything about the locked room, sir?" Martin asked.

"Why, is one of the rooms locked?"

Martin described the location to him, and he said, "Oh, that would be the cedar room, where all the blankets and woolen clothes were stored. But it was never kept locked. Madam must have put some other things there for safekeeping." His cheeks flushed boyishly, his eyes were happy behind his glasses. "The chess set must be there, and some of the other things I haven't found. Though really one would have expected her to put the Lowestoft up there, if she didn't want to bother to have it packed and taken away. Of course, in spite of her protestations she probably intended to come back eventually. Madam was like that . . . ." He dreamed a little, and Monica wondered what he was seeing. Then he returned eagerly to the present. "The Brices must have the keys . . . . mustn't they?"

"They haven't, sir," said Martin, "and Homer says his grandfather gets furious if it's mentioned. He feels it was a slur on his honesty not to leave the keys."

"Dear me, then, I shan't—er—upset him. But I hope those keys aren't locked away and—er—forgotten in a safety-deposit box somewhere."

With the dishes out of the way and beds made, Martin and Monica went to the cove to wait for Homer. The morning was calm, though a light velvety breeze occasionally brushed their cheeks. Presently a high-powered roar heralded *The Blue Streak,* which came around the point between two splendid bow waves like great white

87

wings, and headed straight for the shore. A little distance from the beach Homer shut off the outboard and stood up. The boat glided toward them on a soft rush of water and nosed the sand.

"Look, Ma, no hands," said Homer with a grin. "How's that? Like to see you do that with a sail."

It was fun after all, skimming over the bright smooth water, snaking through the confetti spatter of pot buoys, waving at the lobster boats they passed. In what seemed a very few minutes they were slipping along under a mainland shore, the engine slowed down so they could see the tidy wharves, the anchored sailboats and speedboats of the summer people, the comfortable houses set on vivid green lawns backed by spruce woods. Sometimes someone was fishing off a float, or getting ready for a day's sailing, and Homer called to them by name, and they waved and shouted back at him.

These people looked so *sure*, Monica thought. That long-legged girl in white shorts was probably just what she seemed, happy and unworried as she began a day's fun, knowing she was where she was supposed to be, where she had a *right* to be . . . Quite suddenly and fiercely Monica resented the girl, who had taken all the shine out of the morning, and she had to work to recapture a good mood.

Homer took them around Port George harbor, among yachts, sardine carriers, fishing boats, an anchored seaplane. Then they were out around the far point, heading away from mainland as if straight for Spain. A little light wind flicked the water into bright crests. Heading across them made the boat seem to go faster, almost to

88

fly. Martin was steering now and his face was set in an expression of sheer joy. Monica looked back at him with amusement, and then saw directly behind them another speedboat traveling much faster, so that water kept flying up and pouring over the bow and sides in white curtains of spray. Someone stood up, leaning on the windshield as the boat hurtled on.

"Look!" she called to Homer, who snapped his head around. "Could they overrun us?" He scowled angrily at the oncoming boat. Martin gave a quick glance over his shoulder, then turned his attention back to steering again.

"Just a wise guy," Homer shouted at Monica. "Trying to scare us. I know him. Slow down!" he signaled to Martin, who obeyed. Now they could hear the high-pitched whine of the bigger outboard motor and the splash of the bow waves. The boat slowed abruptly and bobbed toward them. She was white, lapstrake, with a varnished deck, a wide double seat, and many flashing chrome fittings. She looked much the same as the boat they'd seen shooting away from the island the other day. As she came alongside, both Homer and Martin reached out to hold her off so neither boat would scrape the other.

A thin tall sandy-haired boy looked down over the windshield at them, unsmiling under a duck-billed cap, his mouth pulled in tightly, his eyes—which were also sandy-colored—in a wide expressionless stare. Homer said reluctantly. "Hi, Pooch. What do you want?"

"I was looking for you." Pooch hardly moved his pale lips.

"Oh." Homer looked off to sea while the two boats

rocked gently. Monica tried to pretend she wasn't there, but Martin grinned cheerfully at the antisocial Pooch.

"You were really traveling. How fast does she go?"

Pooch ignored him and stared at Homer's ear, which had turned quite red. Suddenly he swung his head around and blurted, "I told these kids I'd take 'em for a spin. I'll be ashore this afternoon. What's the hurry? You taking off for San Francisco or something?"

Pooch lifted one shoulder and one side of his mouth to match. "It just so happens that when I get a job for a feller I expect him to show some interest."

"I told you I'd be in later," Homer said belligerently.

For the first time Pooch smiled; at least it was an upward turn of his lips at both ends. "Don't you believe in introducing folks, Homer?"

Homer, obviously suffering, mumbled, "Monica Sanborn, Martin Sanborn, Pooch Robey."

Martin stood up to shake hands. Monica said, "Hello, Pooch."

"Hi, there!" said Pooch, now permitting himself a flashing grin, which she was sure he had practiced before a mirror, along with the tight-lipped impassivity which had preceded it. "Well, Homer," he said jovially, "you get all the clutter out of the way before you start this job. Okay?"

"Okay," Homer muttered.

"See you," said Pooch with a nod at the others, and started up his engine, reversed with a great roaring and foaming, and headed back toward the mainland. *The Blue Streak* rocked in his wake.

"Is that the kind of engine you want, Homer?" Martin asked.

As if in a dream Homer said, "Twenty-five horse. Yep, that's the baby."

"What does Pooch do?" asked Monica. Besides rushing around looking inscrutable, she wanted to add. "Go to school, go fishing, or what?"

"Oh, he's like me, does whatever he can turn his hand to."

"Well, he must find plenty that pays off, by the looks of that boat and engine," said Martin.

"Ayuh." Homer seemed to shake himself, and became brisk and assertive. "Better let me take her now, Marty, there's ledges around here and it's breezing up some." As the boys changed places a little gust ruffled Monica's hair, and she could see the darkening trail of breeze across the water. *The Blue Streak* seemed suddenly small and very low-sided as a crest slapped loudly against the hull.

"Maybe we should be starting back," she suggested.

Homer grinned at her. "This isn't anything! Just enough to make it more fun. I can show you a real ride now."

Monica glanced at Martin, but he looked eager enough, so she decided she was being timid for nothing. Homer pulled the starting cord and the boat leaped forward across the sparkling crests. Wind poured in a cold stream against their faces, and spray flew high. As the chop deepened the flat bottom spanked hard, sometimes with an unpleasant jar. The boys seemed perfectly

91

happy, but Monica was not enjoying herself. The sensation of effortless speed was gone, the big clouds billowing up darkly from the horizon meant more wind, she knew that much.

She realized she was holding herself in a tense knot and tried to relax, only to be almost bounced off her seat as the boat dropped into a hollow. She wanted to turn and cry to Homer, "Let's go back!" But he knew what he was doing, knew what his boat could take, knew these tides and winds . . . She set her jaw and stared between the constantly curving falls of water.

Then she saw a low island lying ahead, just a long wavy strip of green growth and tawny rock, surrounded by light surf. She turned her head toward Homer and pointed at the island, and he nodded. "That's where we're going!" he shouted.

They landed on the lee side, on a scrap of sand amongst the boulders. From here, the mainland and Sea Island's group all blended into a greenish-blue mass, seeming much farther away than it really was. From the other side of the low green ridge came the smack, roll, and swash of a rising sea that turned from aquamarine to slate-blue and then to jade streaked with white as the cloud masses sailed across the sky.

"They call this place John's Mistake," Homer explained. "This feller John brought a girl out here to propose to her, and she turned out to be such a battle-ax he was sorry for the rest of his life."

"If you want to propose to my sister," said Martin, "I'll go sit behind a rock."

"Heck, no, I can't afford to get married yet." Homer grinned. "Nope, I wanted to show you the wreck of a big schooner that ran ashore here fifty years ago. Come on."

They followed him through a litter of driftwood tangled with purple-blooming beach peas and pink morning glories to where surf broke over the great sun-bleached ribs. They were half buried in beach rocks that shifted and rattled as the water drew back each time. It was an impressive sight, but Monica wished it had been closer to Sea Island. *The Blue Streak* looked about as imposing as a shingle down there on the sand, and the water between here and home was now dark and seething under a heavy cloud.

"Yep, that was a night," Homer was saying. "You get Gramp to talking. He was a little kid then, but he remembers." He came up to where Monica stood and put his hand on her shoulder. "What are you thinking about?" His eyes smiled into hers. She thought, You *would*, now that I'm so nervous I can't give you my full attention. This is no place for charm, you idiot.

"It looks rough," she said, "and it's dark in the west now as well as in the south. Or isn't this anything?" she added lightly.

He stared around them, and whistled. "By gorry! I never thought it'd breeze up so fast!"

Martin joined them. "Do we wait for it to flatten out? Will it do that when the tide turns?"

"Trouble is, it's likely to keep breezing on like this till dark." His forehead creased deeply. "I'd never have

93

taken a chance if I'd guessed. Weather report said five-to-ten knot wind, but this is getting up to twenty—twenty-five, mebbe more."

"What do you think we should do?" Monica asked with measured calm.

"Only thing I can think of is for me to go in alone, and get somebody to come out for you. She'll bounce along over this like a chip with just me aboard, and I'll get a feller from the Port to come out. Heck, this'll be nothing to a lobster boat."

"Maybe you'd better not try." Martin was beginning to be nervous now. "You'll have a following sea rolling up under your stern all the way. Wouldn't they start looking for us pretty soon? Pooch saw us coming out—he'd tell."

"Pooch is likely to have taken off in his car and be half-way to Bangor or somewhere by now. No, I better go." He started down to his boat. "Just so long as you two don't get scared foolish."

"What of?" asked Monica crisply. "We'll be on dry land. The only thing to worry about is you."

"Oh, I've been out in worse than this."

A strong gust hit Monica's back and pushed her forward. Martin got a splash of spray from a wave breaking over the timbers. "Hey!" he shouted, half-laughing. "This place doesn't go under at high tide, does it?"

"Once in a while, if it's storming at a floodtide." He was untying the boat, and he straightened up. "Oh, my gorry, I dunno if we're having short tides now or eleven footers. I'd better dust out of here some fast and get hold of somebody."

94

Martin took hold of the other side of the boat and they dragged her down into the water, which swirled around the stern and splashed aboard. Now the lee was choppy as the wind struck down across the islet. It seemed to come from several directions at once, snapping around in an unpleasantly whimsical way. Up to his knees in the bubbling water, steadying *The Blue Streak* while Homer got aboard, Martin said—too casually—"This weather acts pretty funny to me."

"You don't know how funny our weather can be, chummy." Homer laughed. He seemed excited by the wind, the thickening and rushing clouds, the flying spray. And not too worried about leaving us here, Monica thought crossly, then stifled the notion as unfair and unkind.

"Oh, I don't know about that." Martin managed to look positively bored. "I've seen some darned peculiar weather here and there, and whenever it acted like this it meant trouble."

"Well, it's too early for hurricanes." Homer braced himself by the engine. "Give me a good shove out, and don't stub your toe and drown yourself."

Martin obliged, and Homer, still grinning, turned to tip the engine down into place. Suddenly the boat rolled down on one side and water swept in over the gunnel and swashed over the engine. Homer was taken off balance and almost lost his footing. By the time he'd steadied himself, *The Blue Streak* had slewed around sidewise to the surge, and the propellor of the outboard was hitting against a boulder.

Homer wasn't grinning now. Frantically he tried to

95

right the boat with an oar thrust overboard, but the way between the rocks to open water was too narrow, and once the boat was rolling across it, every movement only made her or the engine hit in another place. Besides that, she was almost completely swamped in no time; the seat cushions, the other oar, Homer's jacket, and some other miscellaneous objects, were beginning to float out.

It was all too fast for Martin and Monica to feel anything. The thrusting oar wedged in a crack and snapped, and the boat was sinking. Homer jumped overboard, swearing, but Martin's shove had sent the boat out beyond Homer's depth, and the expression of horror on his face as he went down turned Monica sick. The yellow head bobbed up from the foam and was almost struck by the propellor. His hands reached for the side of the boat and she sank under their grip.

The two watching splashed simultaneously into the water. "Be careful!" they yelled to each other, feeling the force of the undertow pulling at them. Monica's foot skidded on rockweed and she almost went down, but righted herself. Martin grabbed at a retching and swearing Homer who swung out madly in all directions. Monica seized one of the flailing arms, shouting, "You're all right!"

He gave her an aghast look from bloodshot eyes, then a weak grin. "Okay, okay!"

The three stumbled ashore, Homer in the middle, and then Martin went back to salvage anything he could. An ominous sound brought the sodden Homer to his feet in anguish, but *The Blue Streak* was already splintered along her port side, and she'd come down hard on a sharp point of rock that went through the bottom. Homer sank back again, head on his knees, and Monica was torn between pity for him and her desire to be out there splashing around with Martin. It had got very dark again, and she thought she felt spatters of rain, but it could have been spray. The air was very warm, it could have been blowing directly off hot fields and forests rather than across water.

"Eureka!" Martin howled in triumph. He had grabbed the shaft of the engine at an instant when the sunken hull shifted lengthwise into the passage among the boulders, and was holding onto it with all his strength against the pull of the water. Monica jumped up and waded in to help him. The water-filled boat was heavy and balky, and the surge fought them like a living enemy, but in a few minutes they had her beached out stern-first on the sand, with waves breaking over the bow.

Revived by the sight, Homer was there to unscrew and unchain the outboard from its mount. He and Martin carried it up onto the grass, then heaved *The Blue Streak* up farther on the sand and turned her over. The shattered edges of the wood showed bright yellow against the blue paint, and Homer stood staring at the wounds with an unreadable expression.

"Well, old son," said Martin. "I guess you're not going anywhere."

Homer tried for a grin. "For a minute there I thought I was going straight to the bottom of the sea." He ran his hand over the splintery gashes. "Maybe Gramp can fix

97

her. As long as the engine's all right, that's the main thing."

"And you being alive after being swamped," said Monica. "That's an important little item."

"Thanks. Some folks wouldn't think so."

"Why?"

He shrugged. "Too long a story to go into now. We'll save it for a special occasion when we haven't got a chaperone."

"I offered to sit behind a rock," said Martin, "but I want one that the tide doesn't come up to. Were you just kidding when you said you didn't know if this would be a short tide or an extra high one? Just giving the greenhorns a scare?"

Homer's face changed. "By gosh, I *don't* know. I should, but I don't. Look, let's start collecting a mess of this dry driftwood and get a big fire going. Somebody'll see it all right. There'll be fellers coming in from hauling, yachts, draggers going by outside . . . Sure, somebody'll see that fire right off."

"Who's got matches?" Martin asked.

"Where's that tin box I saw you make a grab for?" He took it up and pried off the lid. "See, I'm all ready for a shipwreck, except from now on I'll keep some sardines and candy bars in here." There was a first aid kit, and matches in a plastic container.

They began cheerfully to gather wood, calling back and forth when somebody discovered a good pot buoy or a shattered trap with new nylon heads in it, or some other treasure. I suppose this is really an adventure to enjoy,

98

Monica thought. With all the traffic there is on a summer afternoon we'll be picked up long before high tide . . . . Here she gave an apprehensive glance around her. The islet was growing steadily shorter and narrower. Yet the coarse grass, the wild flowers, and the dry driftwood proved that the tide didn't go over the island very often. If only they could be *sure* of this time . . . I will remember this day all my life, she thought. And part of the memory would be the way Homer had looked when he said, "Some folks wouldn't think so." Just recalling it now, as she went along above the gleaming surf in the darkening light, gave her a queer wrench of compassion.

It was as if Homer didn't really belong anywhere, and she knew what that was like. He never mentioned his parents, yet he didn't stay all the time with his grandparents as if they were raising him . . . Right now he stood alone at one end of the islet, against stormy sky and boiling seas, and she saw him like that in his life, lonely, solitary, wanting desperately to have things of his own, like a more powerful engine to make him *somebody*.

We're something alike, she thought, except that Martin and I have each other. If anything ever happened to Martin I'd die. I thought Homer was lucky because he has grandparents, but if it's his father he really wants, or a brother, he can still be lost.

She straightened up with her arms full of dry wood, and looked toward the mainland. She saw lightning streak and flicker through the western sky, and just barely audible above the water's noise there was the rumble of distant but steady thunder.

99

11

THAT WAS the reason for the hot wind which was drying them off quite efficiently. It was also the reason for Homer's pallor. He too had seen the lightning, and was so obviously upset it was impossible to ignore the subject.

"Do thunder storms make you nervous?" Monica asked him. "They do some people."

"We have some real peelers around here," he said aggressively. "I'm not the only one that doesn't like 'em. Nobody does, unless they're foolish."

"Well, I don't think I like being caught out here in one." Martin tactfully hid the fact that he loved a good, noisy, flashing, roistering thunder storm.

"Maybe it'll go up toward the north, the way it did the other day in the fog," Monica suggested. "I *hope* it will."

"There's likely more than one," Homer muttered, "and if we get our fire going they'll think it was set by lightning out here, and they won't come. That is, if the rain don't put it out."

"Could lightning strike out here?" Monica asked apprehensively.

"It can strike anywhere, can't it?" He darted a glance at the fireworks in the west. The lightning dazzled against a blue-black sky, and the thunder was louder. He wet his lips. Even Martin began to look preoccupied.

"Let's not just stand here," he said briskly. "How about piling up all our wood under *The Blue Streak* to keep dry? We can have our fire after the rain. Somebody ought to be thinking about us by then, so the fire should mean something. Isn't your grandfather likely to call the Coast Guard?"

Homer shot another frightened look at a blue-white flash. "He likely thinks we're on the mainland somewhere."

Monica's stomach knotted. She was aware of fear rising up like a monstrous wave, ready to drown her. "Come on!" she said loudly. "Let's get that wood together! We'll have to lay planks over the holes in the bottom of the boat." She began scrambling around in a fury of activity, Martin joined her, but Homer moved sluggishly, as if his fear had taken his strength.

"I've got a thought," Martin called. "We can make a shelter with some of those old lobster traps. Shake a leg, Cap'n!"

In spite of the twisting in her stomach, Monica felt a new pity for Homer. It was degrading not to be able to hide your fear. And if you were afraid, afraid in your bones and your sinews so you thought your legs wouldn't hold you up or your hands do what you told them to do, there was nothing you could do about it. She knew what it was like; she could never despise anybody for such melting terror, she could only suffer with him.

There was no escaping the storm. It came rapidly across the water with mad billows of wind that turned the sea white and blew the tall grass over flat. The thunder rolled like an artillery barrage, the lightning lit up the world. Helped somewhat by a shaky Homer, the brother and sister built their shelter on the seaward side of the ridge. Desperation gave them the strength to haul *The Blue Streak* across and down over a bank of tough grass. They used the hull for a roof, the side walls were old lobster traps standing on end and banked with thick clumps of rockweed ripped from the shore. They made a thick platform of the salvaged boards and laths and shingles, and crawled in upon it just as the downpour began.

It pounded so loud on their roof that at times they could hardly hear the thunder, but from the open front of their shelter they saw the sea illuminated by the almost constant glare. There were a few snapping, crackling explosions as if giant boulders were being dropped on *The Blue Streak,* and Homer's utter silence as he sat between Martin and Monica took on a frightening quality.

"I'm cold," Monica said. "Aren't you cold, Homer, Martin? Let's all put our arms around each other." She had to unclamp his hand from his knee and put his arm around her waist, where it tightened into a rib-squeezing grip. She and Martin each wrapped an arm around Homer, and he gave in at last to the shudders he'd been trying to suppress. The other two talked about everything they could think of. Their throats went dry and their voices went hoarse, and Monica tried not to think how thirsty the sight of all that rain made her.

Their inventiveness began to weaken from sheer fatigue as one shower succeeded another. At each flash of lightning Homer jumped as if it had pierced his body.

Then one of the others would say, "Remember that time in Such-and-such when you did So-and-so?"

And then it was over. The rumble was far away to the east, the lightning flashed out over the horizon, the rain had stopped and the silence was the most *silent* Monica had ever heard. They loosened their aching arms and crawled out into a damp and aromatic dusk. Stars were beginning to show, and the mainland lights trembled like more stars.

"Well," said Homer in a normal voice. "Seems like it's gone. Tide's gone some too. Must have been a short one."

"I'm hungry," said Martin. "Let's draw lots to see who gets roasted first." They all laughed. Nobody made reference to Homer's silent, shaking terror. In relief that the storm was over and the tide hadn't flooded them out, they were all noisy and cheerful as they carried the dry wood to the top of the ridge. Homer started the fire in a handful of dry chips, and they kept adding to it until they had a blaze which both warmed them and seemed to illuminate the whole night. Except for being ravenous, they were comfortable, even relaxed.

In a little while they heard the sound of a big engine and Homer was able to separate a vessel's riding lights from the sparkle of mainland ones.

"It's Mont Cady," he said jubilantly. "I know that engine. He's out looking for herring."

The sound grew louder, the lights bright, and soon the forty-five foot seiner stopped offshore and someone shouted, "Is that a distress signal or a weenie roast?"

"Distress!" Homer yelled back. "My boat's wrecked!"

"Is that you, Homer? You got a girl with you out there?"

"And her brother," Homer called.

"Shucks, that's no way to go getting wrecked!"

A man rowed a dory across the now-tranquil approach and collected them and Homer's engine. "I'll get Pooch to bring me out to get the boat," he said. "We'll patch her up enough to tow."

Aboard the big boat they were given sandwiches and mugs of strong coffee in the crowded cabin, and subjected to a lot of good-natured teasing. Monica thought that the weather-browned faces of the crew were the handsomest she'd ever seen. Not until now, when safety was no longer a dream, would she admit to herself that the experience on the islet had been an ordeal.

And Homer would hate them now because they knew how frightened he had been . . . She looked slyly across the cabin at him to see if he had changed. He was joking with the captain, a big, amiable, young man, and seemed not to have a care in the world. Suddenly he caught her eye and gave her the usual wink. She smiled, surprised by the strength of her relief.

Martin was outside with the man at the wheel, and Monica went out there too, standing in the lee of the canopy and watching through the windshield as the land separated in the starlight into dark clumps of islands. The boat found her way along the pale glimmering canals, cutting the water into ruffles of greenish-white fire and leaving behind a broad and luminous wake. Suddenly lamplit windows shone out at them, and the fire-fly spark of a flashlight. The engine slowed to a soft pulsing and headed toward the Brices' wharf.

The dogs barked hysterically as the big boat slid alongside the spilings. "What you doing out here, Mont?" Mr. Brice called. "Haven't brought any more Sanborns, have ye? They all seem to be flying back to the nest." Then, as his flashlight rested on Homer's engine, lying across the stern, he said in a different voice, "Where's the boy?"

"Safe enough, Gramp!" Homer came up from the cabin.

"Brought you three derelicts, Elmore," said Mont. "They sat out the storm on John's Mistake."

"I thought all three were waiting it out snug on the main," Mr. Brice said grimly. "Good thing we never had no idea of the truth. Cora'd like to died of worry. Much obliged, Mont."

"Oh, it wasn't any trouble. They had some big old fire going, and we thought we was going to a weenie roast."

"From now on," said one of his crew, "that place will be known as Homer's Mistake."

The castaways climbed up on the wharf, fending off the dogs' passionate greetings. The outboard was handed up, more thanks were offered, and then the seiner left with a whale's smooth grace. They walked up to the house, Homer explaining briefly that *The Blue Streak* had swamped in a sudden squall. By silent agreement the others didn't add to the story. A person had a right to save his pride any way he could.

"You'd better not give your grandmother any details

and get her all fussed up," Mr. Brice said sternly. "Just say Mont brought you home, and that's enough."

Mrs. Brice and Uncle Theo were playing cribbage. She wanted to feed them at once, but Martin and Monica told her they'd already eaten and wanted only to go to bed.

"I'll go with you, dear children," said Uncle Theo. "I must admit I've been here since the first mutter of thunder. Sea House seems to present too tempting a target, in spite of all the lightning rods." He smiled at Mrs. Brice. "You'll be glad to be rid of me."

She flushed and showed dimples. "Lordie no, Mr. Sanborn! I've enjoyed it!"

Walking home through the wet woods they told Uncle Theo where they'd spent the storm and why, leaving out Homer's fright. He was suitably impressed, and promised not to mention it to Mrs. Brice. It was rather nice to have somebody older to tell things to, Monica thought, and she knew by the way that Martin was talking that he appreciated it too. Uncle Theo was nothing like their father, but he was kind, and appeared to have a genuine affection and concern for them. We'll enjoy it while we can, she decided grimly, because it can't last forever.

"Now," said Uncle Theo in the kitchen. "Go and get out of those damp clothes, and I'll build a fire and make something hot to drink. It feels like autumn since the wind changed."

It feels like autumn. Monica shivered, but not with cold. What would autumn bring?

In pajamas and robes they returned to the kitchen to drink cocoa at the kitchen table. "You two children have had quite a day," Uncle Theo said, "and so have I, in a far less strenuous, though perhaps more disturbing way." He stopped to light his pipe and they sipped the boiling cocoa and tried not to look too eager, though Monica was sure they shared the same thought. When he began again, sadly, they didn't dare look at each other.

"So many things that I remember are missing. They must be scattered all over the country, and I can't help feeling some resentment. I'm sure none of the present owners can have half the love for those objects that I have."

"Did you ever think that things could have been stolen out of the house instead of given away?" Martin looked innocent and handsome by lamplight. Monica tried to find his foot to kick, but he'd prudently tucked both out of reach.

"Stolen?" Uncle Theo was shocked. "Oh, no, dear boy! Certainly not here!"

"Well, some mainland houses have been broken into."

"But this is Sea House on Sea Island," said Uncle Theo, like one saying, But this is Buckingham Palace.

Martin kept quiet after that, but Monica remembered that they were supposed to be listening for noises at night, and they'd forgotten about getting the dogs in. By now she was so groggy from her day nothing seemed important but bed. Her eyelids were so heavy she kept blinking to keep them from closing altogether.

"You'd better go to bed, dear girl," Uncle Theo said. "You run along too, Martin. I shall sit here and smoke a while and—er—cogitate."

They might have been eight and ten, instead of fifteen

and seventeen. But they said good night and went upstairs with their flashlights, and Monica had a vision of what it would be to live forever in a place like Sea House with somebody like Uncle Theo for a guardian. It was a mad dream, and it would not erase the awful reality of Aunt Naomi. Drooping, she turned in at her door.

"Keep listening," Martin said through a convulsive yawn. "I wish we hadn't forgotten the dogs."

"They didn't come with us, that's why we forgot them. I can't listen for anything, Martin. I'm going into a coma." But she compromised by keeping her door open, though she was sure that anyone could steal her bed without waking her.

12

BUT SHE DID wake up, completely alert, to the fact that someone was in her room. She knew at once where she was, and that the someone was Martin.

"Somebody's up in the attic, and it's not Uncle Theo," he whispered. "They're trying to be quiet, but they dropped something."

She pulled on her robe and tiptoed out into the hall with him. At first she could hear only her rapid heartbeat, and then faintly but unmistakably the evidence that someone was moving around upstairs. You could almost doubt that you'd heard anything, but it was there.

"I'm going up," Martin whispered in her ear.

Alarm shook her. "Have you got that pistol?"

"No, *no!* I forgot it. But I've got my light, and I'm going to get a look at him."

Monica fought an impulse to haul him back with both hands and all her weight, and said tensely, "Let's go."

On the narrow stairs to the attic, elbows begged to be bumped with reverberating thuds and every step creaked. They stopped several times to listen; once they heard a definite sound, as of a small object falling, and Martin whispered, "Dropped his false teeth."

Monica was shaken with wild laughter which she had a hard time stifling. Upstairs at last, hardly breathing, they flashed the light into the billiard room, the playrooms, around and over the stacks of cartons and rows of trunks. There was nothing moving here. But like a homing creature the dancing light came to rest on the locked door, and stayed. The two stood staring at the circle of radiance as if it could penetrate the panels and show them what lay beyond.

The sounds had come from there. There was no getting around it. Martin said loudly, "There must be mice up here, that's all I can think of."

"Ghosts," suggested Monica, with a very realistic giggle. "Let's get out of here before I scare myself to death."

This gave them an excuse to hurry downstairs with a normal amount of confusion, though they were careful to go quietly by Uncle Theo's room, and down the front stairs. In the hall Martin whispered, "He must have gone up the back way, and he's got a key into that room. Come on. We'll meet him at the foot of the stairs."

"Right!" Monica agreed, assuring herself that they could blind him with the flashlight in case he had a gun.

As they entered the kitchen Martin shut off the light, and for a moment the blackness was a solid wall close to their noses. Then it thinned, and the windows became pale rectangles spangled with stars. The two started cautiously across the big room, remembering the malice of chair legs, and then were startled into immobility by a thumping confusion on the back stairs. Whoever it was didn't care if he were heard, he cared only about getting out of the house.

Martin threw himself at the kitchen door and

wrenched it open, to the crash of an outer door slamming. Monica joined him in the fresh cool night. He flashed his light in a wide arc but they saw nothing, and the soft rush of the wind through the spruces masked any footfalls. They ran around to the front of the house, furious at being cheated, and started down over the ledges to the shore with a reckless disregard for the possibility of falls and broken bones. The snarl of a big outboard sprang up from the cove and they could tell by the echoes when the boat shot out by the point. Somewhere along the shore toward Brices' the dogs set up a warning clamor.

"Well, he certainly didn't come *in* under power," Martin panted. "Or else he just idled along for a while, and then shut her off and paddled in. If nobody else heard him, the dogs would have started up when he was still a mile away."

"They're noisy pooches if nothing else," Monica agreed. Her skin went cold, then prickled back to life. *"Pooch,"* she breathed.

"What?" Martin sounded depressed. "Let's go in. This wet grass feels like a snowbank."

"Wait a minute!" Monica whispered fiercely. "Pooch. Homer's sulky friend. Didn't that boat of his look like the one we saw around here the other day?"

"A lot of them look like that." He started for the house. It reared high against a rich sky of stars. The sound of the big outboard was dying away toward the mainland. Monica was now conscious of the prickly juniper and thistles they'd ignored during the chase.

"But it *could* be Pooch," she argued. "He's a friend of

Homer's so he'd know the dogs all right. I hope it isn't Pooch, really, because Homer would feel terrible, but I can't help this hunch."

It was affecting Martin now. Once they were in the kitchen they sat by the still-warm stove with their bare feet on the oven hearth, and whispered about it. "Maybe it is . . . Well, supposing. . . . How do you explain this key business? Whoever it is was in that room, so he had a key. . . . They can make impressions and have keys made. . . ."

Finally Martin smacked one fist into the other palm. "I could take one lock off, if we could be alone in the house long enough. But we've got Uncle Theo, dear girl."

"We should tell Uncle Theo what's going on," Monica said stubbornly.

"*No!* Didn't we make a deal about that?"

"I never agreed to anything, I didn't have time. Uncle Theo came along just then."

"Silence gives consent, and you never said anything afterward."

"You're—" She stopped, frustrated, furious with him and herself too. She *hadn't* said anything afterward; she just hadn't thought about it. But an excuse was not a reason, as their father used to tell them.

"Look," Martin wheedled, "let's figure out a way to get into the cedar room, and then when we have a lot of facts to present to Uncle Theo, we'll do it. Right now we haven't got anything at all except what we suspect."

"Well—" She tried to be objective. "All we're sure

112

about is the chess set, that's true. We don't know anything about the Royal Doulton figurines, and the dueling pistols, and the little French clock that should have been in Madam's room, and everything else Uncle Theo's mentioned."

"But we've no way to prove that we don't know anything about those things . . . Of course I'm not saying they may be in the cedar room. Maybe Madam did give them away. Or maybe they've been stolen and sold. But somebody's got a good reason to get into that room, and I want to know what it is."

"Well, we can't do anything more tonight, and I don't think he'll be back," said Monica. "Let's go to bed. We may wake up full of bright ideas in the morning. I always think best then."

The morning, though a dazzler in itself, brought no bright ideas. Monica got out of bed quickly and went straight to the attic to look around, and found Martin already there, studying the lock. "I could take the hasp off with a screw driver. Can't you get Uncle Theo out for a long walk?"

"Anything for the cause," she said. "I'll try."

But there was no need to try, because at breakfast Uncle Theo announced with boyish anticipation that the light north-west wind was perfect for sailing, and if they weren't going to use *Undine* he'd take her out. "Would either of you like to come with me?" he asked belatedly.

"Not me, thank you, sir," said Martin. "I'd like to, but there's some work I've put off for too long."

113

"Fine sense of responsibility, dear boy," Unce Theo praised him, and Martin looked virtuous. "And you, my dear?"

"I'm like Martin, I have to buckle down to some chores. But thank you. Shall I pack a lunch for you?"

"Would you, dear child?" He was touchingly grateful.

They saw him off from the cove, the red sail brave in the morning light, and rushed back to the house like two eight-years-olds let out of school. Martin collected an assortment of screwdrivers and chisels and went up the back stairs.

"You don't need to stand there and breathe down my neck." He was sharp-tongued with nervous tension.

"Who'll hold the screws, then? They'll be rolling downstairs."

"Put your handkerchief down on the step and I'll keep the screws on that. You can go out and fend off anybody you see coming."

She departed with dignity, not a minute too soon. The dogs came racing out of the woods and Homer was behind them. She called back upstairs in a revoltingly cheerful voice, "Mar-*tin!* Here comes Homer!" She went out, and from behind her came a muffled but plainly enraged exclamation; feet pounded down the stairs, a drawer in the kitchen was pulled out and slammed shut, and she knew he was hiding his tools away under the dishtowels.

Homer looked very chipper in new chinos and a sea-blue jersey. "Hi! Any bad effects from yesterday?"

"No, it did me good," said Monica. "How are you?"

"Finest kind. Where's Brud?"

"If you mean me, I refuse to answer," said Martin from the door behind them. "Hi, George. Hi, Babe. *You* wouldn't call me Brud, would you?"

"All right, Your Highness," said Homer.

"Sh!" Martin put his fingers to his lips and rolled his eyes madly. "Even the walls have ears, and I'm supposed to be here incognito. Uncle Theo may turn out to be an agent of the Revolution."

"Too bad," said Homer to Monica. "He was a nice feller before he lost his marbles. Hey, how about putting my engine on the dory and going over to Kestrel? You can find arrowheads and spearpoints, stuff like that, over there."

They were both tempted. In fact it was bitterly hard to refuse. But the chess set had disappeared when they'd both been away for the day before . . . Monica said with real sadness, "I'd love to go, but I can't today."

"Neither of us can," said Martin. "The time has come, old son, to heed the call of duty."

"What duty?" Homer was skeptical.

"Latin. American history. Differential calculus."

Monica thought he was overdoing it and said, "He's just showing off. He's barely into geometry."

"That stuff," said Homer with contempt. "Why spoil a summer's day with it?"

"Because if I don't," said Martin, "there'll come a day in September that'll be worse than spoiled."

Homer shrugged and looked indifferent, but Monica

115

knew he was disappointed. "Well, I don't have to study, but I have to do some baking and ironing," she invented rapidly. "And you could stay around and talk to me if it wasn't too boring for you."

He brightened like the sun emerging from a cloud, but she didn't dare look at Martin. She could feel his wrath. "Martin can go and work for an hour," she said sweetly, "and then we'll have a snack."

"That's just dandy," said Martin with dangerous politeness, and stalked out of the kitchen.

Baking had been the farthest thing from her mind this morning, and she tried now to think what she could make with her limited supplies. She decided on plain vanilla wafers, though in her present mood she expected to turn out something resembling cement chips. Homer was no help. After his blithe start he coasted into a glum silence. Wherever she moved in the kitchen she felt his morose gaze, and it made her self-conscious. She tried to make spirited conversation which came out sounding inane. Homer plunged deeper into his mood. And upstairs Martin was probably simmering away, unless he'd sneaked out the front way and was getting some pleasure out of the brilliant morning. This possibility made her sigh with exasperated envy, and Homer said at once, "What's that for?"

"Oh, I was just wishing I could stay here forever," she improvised, blushing at the fib.

"When do you have to go away?"

"Soon, I'm afraid."

He said belligerently, "I thought you were here for the summer."

116

"I wish we were!" She wasn't lying now. "But we have to get settled down to living with our aunt and getting ready for school, and so forth."

Homer went to the window and stared out, hands in his pockets. After a few moments he said, "I don't know why you had to come at all, if this is all it's going to be."

"That's what I try *not* to think," she said honestly. "But once my brother and I had a dog that lived a long time, and when he died we felt so terrible that I said I wished we'd never had him in the first place. But my father reminded me of all the funny and lovable things, and said, 'Would you want to give up all those things? Aren't you glad you knew Bruno for all those years?' And he was right, because after a while we could stand remembering him without feeling so awful, and we were glad we'd had him."

Homer turned around and faced her. "So?"

"So it's going to be heartbreaking to wake up on summer mornings and know how it looks and smells here, but I'm still going to be glad that I *know* what Sea Island is like." She smiled at him. "And even if I have to wait until I'm making my own living, I'm coming back, even if it's only as far as Port George. The island may be sold by then, and you'll have to take me around it by boat for a long look."

He wouldn't laugh with her. "You won't come back," he said in a colorless voice.

Who went away from him before and never came back? she wondered all at once. "I *promise* you," she began, but the dogs began barking outside, and Homer went out as if he were glad to escape. The dogs subsided and she heard voices. When Homer came in again Pooch was with him. He gave Monica his ineffable flashing grin. Homer stared gloomily at the floor.

"I knew better than to try at the other place for him. I knew he'd be over here where you were."

"You know quite a lot," said Monica demurely.

"I sure do." He leaned over the back of a chair and concentrated on her. Apparently she was supposed to be overwhelmed. "I can tell you're a good dancer just by looking at you. If this punkin-head hasn't asked you to a dance yet, it's because he's got two left feet."

"Now that's something you *don't* know," Monica told him. "Homer's one of the best dancers I've ever met anywhere."

Pooch straightened up. "When'd he have you to a dance? I never saw you at any of 'em."

"We don't need to go to a public place," said Monica in her best cosmopolitan accent. "We have a ballroom here." And you know all about it, you conceited oaf, she thought ungraciously.

"Well, now," drawled Pooch, "I guess old Homer's been having it pretty good, keeping you to himself. But it's time he shared with his best friend. I'm asking you here and now to the dance next Saturday night at Port George."

"Thank you very much," said Monica, "but I have an engagement for Saturday night."

Pooch shot a narrowed glance at Homer, who through some miracle managed to look smug. "Well, I haven't got time to stand around gassing all day," said Pooch curtly. "Come on, Bub."

118

"Don't let anybody involve you in anything for Saturday night, Homer," Monica said as he followed Pooch. He gave her his old grin and wink behind the other boy's back. Feeling as if she'd done a good deed, she watched them start down to the shore, the dogs playing around them. Yes, Babe and George liked Pooch, and the more she saw of him the more certain she was that he was the burglar.

She went out to the front porch and from there she could see the white speedboat shoot out of the cove in a cloud of spray. Back in the hall she happily shouted her brother's name. He came whooping down the bannister, dug out his tools, and rushed up the back stairs. Monica went on with her baking, not taking any chances on being surprised. The dogs lying in the shade of the woodshed were a good warning system. They barked again, stopping when they recognized Mr. Brice coming from the woods.

Martin came down, scowling fearfully. "He probably wants to check something upstairs. Look for holes in the roof or something!"

"Relax and look pleasant!" she hissed at him.

The sun was hot by now, and Mr. Brice was perspiring when he came in. "Homer here?"

"He was, but he just left with Pooch," said Monica.

"They've probably gone out to get *The Blue Streak,*" Martin offered. "Sit down, sir. How about a drink of cold spring water?"

"Gone off with Pooch, has he? I keep hoping the draft board'll catch up with that one, but I guess they don't want him and I can't blame 'em . . . I'll have that drink."

"Would you rather have a cup of coffee?" Monica asked. "And I'm going to take some cookies out of the oven in a minute."

"Haven't the time, girl. I've got wood to saw and get it out of the woods. I counted on that boy, and now he's skinned out."

"Can I help?" asked Martin.

"Darned if I'm not willing to take a chance on ye. Come along."

Waiting for her second batch of wafers to bake, Monica went up herself and studied the lock, wondering if she would get very far with a screwdriver or if Mrs. Brice would suddenly take it into her head to call. She decided not to take a chance.

When all her baking was finished, she went upstairs to tidy her room and change into shorts. Another wonderful day, and what would she do with it? She caught herself humming one of Uncle Theo's tunes; for a moment she was actually the serene and happy and confident girl who *belonged*.

Diagonally across the hall from her room a door that had been closed now stood ajar. This happened often in the house if enough doors were open that the wind could blow up stairways and down passages; other doors clicked open, and she or Martin always latched them again, with no more than a glance inside the room. They had agreed at the first not to be too familiar with the house.

This was definitely a grandmotherly sort of sitting room, where the children were probably lectured, comforted, or threatened with the loss of Madam's esteem.

"May I, Madam?" Monica murmured, and knelt down by the small bookshelf. She glanced swiftly around the room, trying to see all she could in an instant. More sketches and water colors and photographs covered the walls; the whole room was a fascinating collection of objects she would love to examine and handle. She might ask Uncle Theo. Surely his permission would make it all right. She wouldn't open any drawers or cupboard doors, naturally. . . .

That dress form in the corner, now; was *that* Madam's figure? Who was the child in pastels over the mantel? From studying the picture she looked upward, across the low ceiling. . . . and across an oblong indentation in the time-darkened white paint. A *trap door?*

She stood up and stared at the ceiling. Then with one long step she was at the windows. They looked out over the garden site, the rose thickets, and thence to the woods. She knew by the position of a particular clump of lupin that these windows were directly above the kitchen windows. And that meant that the locked cedar room was above this one. And *that* meant—

Her throat drying with excitement, she turned back to the trap door. If that *was* a trap door, and not just a panel set into the ceiling, it must open into the locked room.

She pulled a chair out from the sewing table, tested it for steadiness, and stood up on it. She could reach the indented oblong, but instead of moving it her hands could have been pressing against solid ceiling. Still, she could be almost sure now that it was a trap door, because she could see where the opening came. The crack had been painted over when the ceiling was last painted, but in most places it hadn't filled the crack.

No, a chair wasn't enough, you needed a stepladder so you could get close enough to use more pressure. She put the chair back at the sewing table and went for the stepladder in the woodshed, jubilant with her discovery. Columbus couldn't have been more excited, she thought, and then, with her hands actually on the stepladder, she stopped. She couldn't do anything without Martin. Whatever lay beyond the trap door, they had to find it together.

It was flattening, but only for a moment. At least she'd have a surprise for him when he came back. Singing to herself—Uncle Theo again, she thought with a grin—she fixed her lunch, chose a book, and went out to find a secret place along the shore.

13

IN THE LATE afternoon she gathered mushrooms on the way home, planning supper
and how she would surprise Martin with the trap door
when she got him alone. She stopped to watch a pair of
fishhawks gliding in great effortless circles overhead,
crying to each other. When she lowered her eyes a man
was standing in the path looking at her.

She jumped, and he said quickly, "I'm sorry to startle
you. I was just taking a look around." He was tall, with
attractively rugged features, and he had dark red hair.
He was older than Monica, at least twenty-one, she
guessed. And there was something about him that con-
vinced her she looked stupid, rumpled, uncombed and
unlipsticked. She certainly *felt* that way. He smiled
and said, "Cousin Monica, I believe. I'm Peter Sanborn."

Every bit of feeling seemed to go out of her head, arms,
and legs all at once. She said faintly, "How do you do?"

"I don't really look like Hamlet's father's ghost, do
I?" he inquired. "I'm beginning to wonder. Uncle
Theo looked at me the way you do."

His patronizing manner revived and infuriated her.
Her own smile came, dangerously sweet. "I suppose it's
because we've been so scattered we've come to believe

there really aren't any other Sanborns. I mean, how do we *know?*"

"Exactly," he agreed. "How do we know? The house could be full of imposters, but we'd have no proof of it."

"Gruesome, isn't it?" said Monica. "Well, I'd better see about supper." He walked behind her, and she wished he wouldn't. Her skin twitched, her back felt vulnerable. "Have you met my brother?" she asked.

"Briefly, but he wasn't feeling well and went straight to his room. He'd been hauling wood in the sun all day."

I'll bet he wasn't feeling well, she thought, but not because he'd been hauling wood. "When did you arrive?" she said, wondering how her shorts looked after a skid she'd taken in the rockweed.

"I flew up from Boston this morning and was hanging around the harbor in Port George, waiting for a lobsterman who lives out here to show up. They'd told me about him in the post office. Well, I was watching a sailing dinghy skimming among the moorings, and the lobster buyer told me the skipper was a relative of mine. So I flagged him in, properly astonished him, and here I am."

Here he was indeed, and she'd like to go to bed as Martin had and let him and Uncle Theo find their own supper. She was never going to be able to eat again.

"It's a marvelous place," the annoying drawl went on. "It's everything I wanted it to be, and more. And to find some family here was the finishing touch. Actually I did this on my own hook. I'm supposed to be in South-West

124

Harbor, but I left the plane at Limerock strictly on impulse. I've wanted to see this place all my life, and I didn't think the lawyers would throw me in jail if I simply took a look."

Jail. She felt weak and sick, as if she couldn't take another step. Of course he was exaggerating, it was the form of humor that went with the affected manner ... "If they do, then we'll all be in jail together," she said flippantly, "because none of us has permission."

They came into the kitchen and she remembered with dismay how smug she'd been this morning at putting Pooch in his place, which was more than she was going to accomplish with this one. "I'm going up to see how Martin is," she said, and left, carrying a picture of Peter Sanborn with his hands in his pockets, his eyes gleaming with secret and malicious humor behind the lashes.

Martin was lying on his bed and he sat up when she came in. "Did you see him?"

She nodded, and they stared at each other in a silence that got worse and worse. "What do we do now?" Martin asked bleakly.

"I feel like packing and leaving tonight, except that we'd have to ask Mr. Brice to take us over, and everybody would talk about it. If only we could just fold our tents like the Arabs and silently slip away."

"Listen, you could prove that Uncle Theo was a Sanborn, but how do we know this one is?" demanded Martin. "Did you ever hear of a Peter Sanborn?"

"No, but Father mightn't have known about him. He could be one of those western cousins. Now I've got to

125

get supper. Two of us gone to bed the minute he shows up would be too much. You've got an excuse but I haven't."

"I'll come down if you want me to," Martin said weakly.

"No, you stay here, then I'll have only myself to worry about. And the first thing is to stop looking like a derelict. Did you bring up any wash water?"

"There's some left in the jug."

She took the big flowered pitcher into her room, and poured soft, tepid rainwater into an earthenware basin. She took a quick but thorough sponge bath and splashed on some white-violet cologne. She dressed in a pink-flowered full-skirted lawn dress, applied rosy lipstick, fastened white sandals on her slim, tanned feet. When she went back into Martin's room he whistled.

"Thank you, *m'sieu.*" She dropped a small curtsey. "I'll bring you something suitable for an invalid."

"I'm hungry," he moaned after her. "I've been a lumberman all day. I want some of that pie that Mrs. Brice gave me."

Going down the hall she remembered the trap door. With Peter Sanborn in the house they wouldn't dare prowl around tonight. She met Uncle Theo at the head of the stairs and he gave her a weak, worried smile.

"I brought home some groceries, but I still wish I hadn't sailed into Port George, dear girl."

"How could you know? Besides, if he's a Sanborn he's got a right to be here."

"*If* is an enormous word. I'm not at all sure who he is. He mentioned both my cousin Arthur and my nephew

126

Edward, but I couldn't be sure afterward if he said that he was Arthur's grandson or Edward's son, and one hates to ask, it sounds so hostile somehow." His mouth twitched. "Possibly because I feel hostile. We've been so snug here, the three of us. I hope I haven't brought a cuckoo into the nest."

As always, she wanted to comfort him. "He is supposed to be somewhere else, so perhaps he won't stay very long. And if he hasn't got permission either, he can't very well tell on us."

"That young man," said Uncle Theo portentously, "is an unknown quantity."

He was also a challenge. Monica's moment of weakness had been driven away by defiance. She prepared a supper of creamy scrambled eggs with mushrooms and chives, and a salad from the greens in Uncle Theo's grocery order, tossed with Mrs. Brice's old-fashioned vinegar-and-celery seed dressing. The wild strawberry pie sent home with Martin would be dessert.

But all her exhilaration was gone before supper was over. She wondered if Peter thought she was out to impress him with her pretty dress and good meal. He's so conceited, she thought, he must imagine that if a woman's polite to him she's in love with him. Uncle Theo was working hard to be a host, calling him dear boy and Monica dear girl with charming impartiality, and Monica wanted to shout, Uncle Theo, stop trying! Can't you see he's only laughing at us?

"Did you say you were on your way to South-West Harbor, Peter?" she asked him. "Where is that?"

"On Mt. Desert, and it's a fabulous place for sailing

and just for *being* at this time of year. But so is Sea Island, I know now. So I'm not going on for a week or so, unless we Sanborns engage in a blood feud and kill each other all off before then." He turned to Uncle Theo. "I intend to pay my own way, sir."

"Quite right, dear boy, each of us pays his own way here," said Uncle Theo, and lapsed into weary silence.

"I'll get the dessert," said Monica. "If you don't mind waiting and admiring the view, I'll take a tray up to Martin."

Peter smiled at her and she smiled back, astonished by the depth of her enmity. Upstairs, while Martin began to eat, she said rapidly, "He's staying a week at least. And I found a trap door into the locked room today, but when do we get a chance to open it?"

"Where?" He was shining-eyed.

"In that room near mine that we thought was Madam's sitting room. I'm positive about it. But with this Peter around. . . ." Dejected, she sank onto the foot of his bed. "I don't know. Maybe we should just tell him and Uncle Theo about the whole thing, and get out."

"Over my dead body," said Martin, looking menacing. "Besides, we don't even know if this type has a right to be here. Maybe he's the brains of a gang, and he's out here to keep an eye on things. He could even be a *killer*." At her weary and doubtful expression he said with less drama, "Anyway, we should make him prove he's a Sanborn."

"Oh, Martin," said Monica softly.

"I still don't want to tell him," Martin mumbled.

"Look!" He brightened marvelously. "We'll get him and Uncle Theo out of the house at the same time somehow, I'm sure of it. I can feel it in my bones." You're just trying to convince yourself, she thought sadly, but she didn't discourage him. "Let's give ourselves a couple of days more to find out about the trap door. We can stand him until then, can't we?"

"All right," she said at last. Curiously she felt better, as if they had a goal to work for.

After supper Peter complimented her on the meal and went off for a walk. Uncle Theo offered to help her with the dishes, but she said she'd rather do them alone. Occasionally she heard him moving around in the house, humming to himself. He seemed to be very busy, and was up and down stairs a good deal, but she was too preoccupied to wonder what he was looking for now.

She went to bed earlier than usual, unable to enjoy the dusk. Downstairs Uncle Theo and Peter played chess by lamplight; upstairs the brother and sister talked for a while about their future, and a vast lonelinesss and uncertainty threatened them both like the night creeping in over the sea. Tonight they felt very young and they missed their father exceedingly, though neither mentioned it. But the day had been strenuous enough so that they would sleep in spite of everything.

14

SHE HAD TOLD Peter the night before that usually everybody got his own breakfast, and lunch was a help-yourself snack if people were scattered about on their own affairs.

"That suits me perfectly. I gather we meet at dinner for elevating conversation."

"It's supper here," she said, "and I don't know how elevating the conversation is." She remembered with nostalgia the few evenings alone here with Martin, and then how they'd gotten used to Uncle Theo and found out he could spin them endless stories of the old days at Sea House. There'd be no more of such simple pleasures with *this* one around.

She and Martin took their dawn breakfast down to the cove where they could speak aloud without looking over their shoulders. "I wish Homer would come and repeat his invitation," she said. "I'd go like a shot."

"I'm going to help Mr. Brice again."

"The Brices don't think much of Pooch, do they?"

"No," said Martin. "They've got a feeling, but they can't put it into words."

When he left, very gleefully—or so it seemed—she took off for the woods in another direction before anyone else was up. She had lunch, bathing suit, book, and sketchbook, all in a basket, and a blanket over her arm. She went straight through the woods to the far side of the island, a rugged shore of granite, and of wild roses a deep burning pink within reach of spray.

With real pleasure she established a household for herself in the shelter of three great spruces, and went exploring. Sometimes a yacht or a lobster boat went by, and she saw porpoises playing. The gulls grew used to her, and a flock of baby eider ducks and their parents amused her for a long while. She sketched them, she swam in a little cove with a sandy bottom, she ate and read, and finally slept on the blanket floor of her house among the spruces.

When she woke up, cold and a little sad—she'd been dreaming of her father—someone was on the shore just below her. She lay rigidly still. Martin? Uncle Theo? Homer, looking for her? But he'd have the dogs, and they'd have found her before this.

Whoever it was, he was bending down to pick something up. She heard the tiny rattle of beach pebbles. He straightened up, and the sun struck a dark mahogany glint from his hair. It was Peter. He was examining something in his hand, and he looked very pleased with it, as if he could hardly believe his eyes. It was neither an arrogant nor a patronizing expression, but one of pure wonder and delight. He held the small object up to the sun as if to gaze through it, and when he lowered it he looked straight into her shady house.

She counted on the contrast of deep shadow after bright sun to blind him so he'd miss her. But instead his manner sharpened, focusing on her like a camera, and he said, "Hello!" His voice was warm, full of life. "I've just found something remarkable."

"What is it?" she asked politely.

"A chalcedony arrowhead. It's absolutely beautiful, I've never seen another one like it." He came up to her, holding it out. "Take it, hold it up to the light. It's translucent. And worn only slightly—feel that point. It must have just come out of the bank, maybe when the last storm chewed up the shore."

This was a different Peter from the one she had met yesterday. She could appreciate the beauty of the finely-worked lustrous point, and she let him know it. "What did you say it was made of?"

"Chalcedony." He spelled it.

"I thought that only existed in the Bible. 'The first foundation was jasper; the second, an emerald—' "

" 'The third, a chalcedony,' " he finished with her, and they both laughed, pleased with each other, marvelously free of self-consciousness. "Do you know the rest?"

"I mix them up, but I always loved the look of the words, jasper, topaz, beryl, and so forth."

"I learned them all by heart because I was going to be a geologist."

"*Was?*"

"Well, I still am, and this place is practically Eden for a geologist. I'm so loaded with samples now that if I fell overboard I'd sink."

"Don't let this sink with you." She rubbed the arrowhead gently against her cheek. "It's as smooth as satin."

"That was a labor of love, I'd say. I'll bet he felt bad when he lost it." He put it in a shirt pocket and buttoned down the tab.

"When they find your drowned body," she said, "I'll tell them to look in that pocket."

They laughed again, then suddenly he seemed to chill and stiffen. "I'm sorry I barged in on you, woke you up and so forth. I'll be going along." And as quickly as that he was gone, climbing over the rocks without a backward look. The change was as shocking as a slap. She felt cold, tired, utterly despondent. Why had he come along to this spot at all? It had been perfect until then. Why had he let her think she was at least passable as a human being, and then suddenly behaved as if she were a dangerous female of the spider family? Poison variety, she thought cynically. I suppose that's a compliment, in a way.

She gathered up her things and walked slowly home. A few attractive rocks she'd gathered she left behind; if *he* saw them he'd think she was trying to curry favor. Curry favor. That was a silly expression, and what did it really mean? *Look it up,* said her father's voice, and that kept her mind off Peter Sanborn for a while.

When she reached the house no one was in sight. I'll have to plan supper, she thought without interest. I suppose we'll have to call it dinner while Dear Cousin Peter is here. Perhaps we should have it by candlelight, on the Lowestoft, if Uncle Theo permitted. "Spaghetti à la Reine," she composed. "How does that suit Your Grace? *Pasta con eleganza. Ah, bellissima!*" She stalked into

133

the dining room, chin high, kicked back an invisible train of crimson brocade, and stopped short.

The Lowestoft cabinet was almost empty. There was a tureen left, and a couple of smaller dishes, and that was all. Not even the arrival of Peter had given her a greater shock. It was as if the dishes had been charmed out of sight by a wizard before her eyes. She tried to remember when she had last been in the dining room. She could remember talking to Uncle Theo and handling one of the cups, a few days ago. But everything ran together in her memory.

"But I'm sure of one thing!" she exclaimed angrily. "No one got in here at night and stole that set, piece by piece. It's just not *possible!*"

Her mind churning, she went upstairs to tidy up, then down to the kitchen to see what sort of sauce she could concoct from various cans and bottles. Suddenly there was a scrabble of dog toenails on wood, happy panting sounds, and an ardent clawing at the screen door.

"Where'd you come from?" she asked, letting them in. Homer was coming through the woodshed behind them, and she was really pleased to see him after the incident with Peter. "Hello! Where have you been all day?"

"Around," said Homer, looking enigmatic. He propped himself against the sink, arms folded. "I hear you've got a new boarder."

"Have we!" She blew hard. "Uncle Theo thinks that if he hadn't gone into Port George yesterday, we'd have been all right. But I think *that* one would find a way out here if he had to swim. Underwater," she added.

"I got a look at him today. He stopped in at the house for a drink and Gram's coming to pieces about him. She's been feeding him gingerbread and milk and he's fed her enough sweet talk to choke a cow."

"Well, I haven't heard much of that sweet talk." She peeled onions rapidly to get ahead of the tears.

"Oh, he'll get around to it," said Homer cynically. "And you'll be so-oo happy that he came. He's a real handsome gink with a real fancy accent, just what you're used to."

She spun around and glared, difficult because the onion fumes were reaching her eyes. "Homer Brice! If you came over here to start a fight, you can just go home again."

He shrugged and started for the door, but she caught at his arm. "Wait a minute. I don't want to fight even if you do. Homer, I don't really know why I'm explaining this to you, but I don't like Peter Sanborn and he doesn't like me. You were our friend first, and if you're going to stay away because *he's* here, Martin and I will just have to chase after you."

He tried to keep on looking stolid, but color flowed up his neck and into his face and ears. All at once he took her into his arms and kissed her hard. Between the strong squeeze of his embrace, the fervor of the kiss, and her stinging eyes, her chief sensation was claustrophobia. At the same time she thought, Well, this was what you wanted to know about, but what a heck of a time to find out!

The dogs jumped up on them with such great enthusiasm that Homer finally had to let her go and stood glowering at her.

She put her fingers carefully to her mouth. "I'll have to say a bee stung me. Goodness, Homer, but you're forceful!"

"That all you've got to say?"

"Well, I could swoon, I suppose."

"For Pete's sake, don't do that. I wouldn't know what to do with ye." He grinned.

"I should have had on some of my best perfume. Instead it's Essence of Onion, Number Six."

"Happens I like onions."

She went back to making sauce. "Stay and have supper with us. I use lots of onions."

"Nope. Too many Sanborns could spoil a man's digestion. Except for present company," he added.

"Thank you, sir. Can we go to Kestrel tomorrow to look for arrowheads?"

"You going to lug your cousin along?"

"*No!* But I don't think we can leave Martin behind."

Homer laughed. "We'll make him go sit behind that big rock he's always talking about. Pick you up around nine, huh?"

"Yes, and I'll bring the lunch."

"Finest kind," said Homer with real gusto. He advanced on her and kissed her again, this time with less muscular fervor but with more assurance. Then he winked at her, snapped his fingers at the dogs, and left.

Simmering onions and tiny canned meatballs together, she reflected on the two kisses and their effect. They

136

hadn't been unpleasant, but her knees hadn't melted and her spine gone weak. She hadn't wanted to wrap her arms around him and cling. No, she wasn't in love, and that was a relief. It would be too utterly painful to fall in love with someone knowing you might never see him again. Because even though she'd promised Homer and herself that she would come back to Port George, she knew from experience that you couldn't always keep such promises. Life buffeted you around as the surf tossed driftwood chips, and all you could do was try to keep your chin above water.

Better not to fall in love, she thought sadly. Better to be always ready to move on and not have anything dragging at your heart . . . possessions or people. She felt the hard ache of tears in her throat.

"Why so pensive?" Peter Sanborn stood in the doorway from the front hall. He was smiling. She didn't know whether she liked that smile or not. It wasn't like the one she'd seen on the beach, over the arrowhead. Wondering what expression he'd caught on her face, she burned with angry humiliation from her toes to her scalp.

"I was trying to remember a recipe," she said.

"We'll be prepared for a new delight tonight."

"Don't be. It's spaghetti."

"I'm sure your spaghetti will have the proper Continental accent."

If she hadn't known better, she'd swear there were two of them, and the likable rockhound was still out on the shore somewhere. She wished this one would leave her

137

alone. He disappeared, but returned in a moment with some paper bags and began filling the fruit bowl on the kitchen table with grapes, peaches, and candy bars.

"Our lobsterman neighbor stopped in at Brices' wharf and I thumbed a ride to Port George with him."

"So I see."

"And while I was there," he continued, meticulously poking some sort of ridiculous lollypops among the rest as if he were arranging flowers, "I called my mother and told her what she was missing. So she's defying the law-yers too. She'll be here for the weekend." He looked at her then.

Monica's smile felt painted on, a clown's grimace. "Oh, that's nice! Shall I fix a room for her or let her choose her own?"

"She's a hard-working woman. She'll probably enjoy finding something all ready for her, so you make the choice." He gave her that ambiguous smile again, went out the back door, and began to whistle. The sound was like a flute in the clear air, and she'd have enjoyed it if her stomach hadn't been twisting and her hands shaking. She made herself finish putting the sauce together, left it to simmer, and went upstairs, careful not to run like a fugitive even though she felt like one.

By instinct she stopped at Uncle Theo's door. Not that he could prevent or solve anything, but he should be warned. She heard no sound within. Perhaps he was sleeping. As she tried to decide whether to wake him or not, one of the freak drafts swept up the stairs from the front door, and Uncle Theo's door clicked and swung

138

gently open. She put her head around it and said his name.

There was no sign of him, only a clutter of books, old photograph albums, and clothes dropped casually over the furniture. In the middle of the room stood an open trunk.

Now how had he ever got it down from the attic, and when? Peter must have helped him. Had he enough belongings here to fill a trunk, things that were definitely his own? She supposed that he'd found books, clothing, perhaps even old toys of his. It didn't matter. She shrugged and turned away, but in the instant of turning she'd seen something familiar. But *what?* She was drawn back again by that fatal curiosity. Three steps into the room, and she could see.

She saw a glimpse of green and white porcelain in the open trunk. The lid of a small tureen lay half-wrapped in an old sweater, perched atop a number of lumpy parcels wrapped in ancient clothing. She poked a finger at the odd shapes. The rest of the Lowestoft, she was sure of it.

She backed out, shut the door firmly, and hurried to her room. It was all getting to be absolutely too much. Peter's mother coming, and now this. She was positive, from what Uncle Theo himself had said, that nobody had a right to take away any valuable thing that hadn't been left legally to him.

"Hi!" Martin poked his head in. "What are you seeing in that mirror, ghosts?"

"Worse!" She beckoned him in. "Shut the door and

139

come over by the window. I don't know who's in the house and who's out."

"Can't I clean up first?" He was damp with perspiration, coated with spruce and sawdust. "I want to take a swim before we eat, and wash off the grime of honest toil."

"You've got time," she said grimly. She told him about Peter's mother. His face went blank and he sat down on the window seat, all his buoyancy gone.

"I wish there were a way to get out of here tonight," said Monica. "I hate to admit it, but it's the truth. I've got no more interest in locked rooms, no more valor, no more nerve." She knelt beside him and put her hot forehead against the glass. For the first time she wished he were the older one, ready to take command and make decisions.

"Well, shall I get hold of Homer?" Martin asked her after a moment. "He's back from town and all dressed up like a little gentleman."

"I know it. He's been here, and we planned to go to Kestrel tomorrow.... If we run we'll look sneaky—guilty—"

"I suppose you'd rather be taken by the ear and turned over to whatever the authorities are around here, while Aunt Naomi is sent for," he said icily.

"No, I don't want that!" The very picture brought some of her energy back. "I want to keep my head up and be so calm and dignified when we walk out of here that they won't think of questioning us. I'm going to have a room ready for Peter's mother, with flowers and

140

fruit, and everything. There'll be a nice meal ready to serve. We'll be all packed, and we'll leave on the boat that brought her over."

"And what about that nasty little smile of Pete's?"

"It'll change when we tell him about the locked room." It's not always a nasty smile, she thought with incomprehensible sadness. She sighed. "And there's something else. It's about Uncle Theo." She told him the story. "And heaven knows what else he's got stowed away in there."

Martin shrugged. "Well, he's one of the family, isn't he? Nobody's using those dishes and he's stone-broke. Why shouldn't he sell them for what he can get?"

"But they're part of the estate. I don't know whether it's stealing or not, whether he could get arrested, or what. I hate to leave him to that Peter and his mother without warning."

"Don't say anything. It's not our affair."

"Yes, it *is*. If there's any serious trouble I'll think I could have prevented it."

"You won't even know about it," he said. "So forget it."

"I don't want to tattle on Uncle Theo, but I don't want him to go to prison. He *likes* us, Martin."

"He likes everybody." Martin got up, looking bored and disgusted.

"Oh, go and clean up," she said coldly.

141

15

A T SUPPER Martin really did his part. He talked about his day in the woods and made it sound far more dramatic than it actually could have been. When he ran out of inspiration, Uncle Theo took over, rambling on about Madam and the old days. Peter listened to both with ironic amusement. He was no more the person excited over a chalcedony arrowhead than Uncle Theo was. What is he *thinking?* Monica tormented herself. Why is he secretly laughing?

There'd be no chance to investigate the trap door tonight. Neither Peter nor Uncle Theo intended to go anywhere. Peter came down from the ballroom with a dusty old guitar while they were doing the dishes, and went out into the woodshed to work on it.

"Making himself at home," Martin grumbled.

"He's got a right to, though it kills me to admit it."

The dogs arrived, and they could hear Peter talking to them, and the thump of tails against anything in the way as they responded to his attention.

"Those idiots would be friends with anyone," Martin said bitterly. "Look how crazy they are about Pooch. It just goes to show that dogs can't really tell about people."

Monica was afraid he'd openly show his sulks and his jealousy and give Peter more to laugh at. "Let's go away

142

from the house until dark and then we can go to bed," she suggested. "Let's row the dory around to Brices' so Homer can put his engine on it in the morning. We can stay over there for a while."

"*He'll* probably rush down after us and say *he* wants the dory."

"Possession is nine points of the law," said Monica. "Whatever that means." They left the kitchen silently, sprinted through the front hall and across the porch. There was no sign of Uncle Theo. Before they reached the shore the dogs caught up with them, displaying a passionate delight that made up for their friendliness to Peter. At the beach the dogs splashed around the dory as it was pushed off, and then jumped aboard without invitation. As soon as the dory was out around the point the human brother and sister could pretend it was almost the same as it had been before anyone else came.

At the Brices' landing Homer and his grandfather were on the wharf, inspecting *The Blue Streak,* and Mr. Brice's boat was tied up at the ladder. A fidgety Mrs. Brice stood by, obviously dressed for town. Her only concession to island life was her rubber-soled shoes, and she showed Monica the white pumps she carried in a paper bag. "I'm going to the summer theater at Fremont tonight with my friends! That is, I'm going if these menfolks ever get through brooding over that old boat." She was as pink-cheeked and bright-eyed as a child anticipating Christmas. "My lands, I'm glad Homer wasn't aboard when she got swamped and went on the rocks!"

The two looked properly solemn, which wasn't hard.

They were disappointed to know there'd be no evening spent around the organ and the kitchen table. They felt well and truly deserted. Even Homer was going ashore. But they stood on the wharf with the dogs and waved the Brices out of the cove, smiling bravely. They lingered aimlessly around the shore for a while, skipping flat stones and examining rocks, which only reminded Monica that Peter was going to be a geologist. They went up to the Brices' house and talked to the hens and looked at the garden. Then they walked slowly home, and since a chess game was going on in the living room they said brief good nights and went to their rooms, too dispirited even to talk to each other any more.

But on the island of Kestrel the next day they felt almost natural again. Martin found a perfect stone knife and Monica an almost perfect spear point; Homer picked up several scrapers, made in different materials and sizes. They found a chunk of rock studded with garnets, some petrified clay with the imprints of tiny creatures that had lived thousands of years ago, and one large sea-polished crystal of pale amethyst. I'd like to show these to Peter, Monica thought, if he were that boy on the beach. But he isn't, so I'd die rather than even *mention* these.

They dug clams and cooked them in sea water over a driftwood fire. They swam, and then Martin wandered off to search for more Indian artifacts in a shell-studded bank on the other side of the island. Homer and Monica lay in the sun. She was watching the slow shining creep of the tide up over the dry sand when he said, "What are you thinking?"

"Thinking that I have to soak everything up like one big sponge," she said dreamily. "I can't let anything go by that I see, smell, hear, or touch...What are *you* thinking?"

"Why didn't your mother come with you?" he asked abruptly.

"She wanted to, but she couldn't." It wasn't a lie. "I told your grandmother."

"I know what you *said*." He was staring steadily at the water. "But I thought maybe she'd just—you know—gone away somewhere on her own."

"No. She'd never go away from us of her own free will." Her words echoed in her ears. She turned her head toward Homer. "Why'd you ask? Did *your* mother—?" She was instantly ashamed for asking, but Homer gave her a sleepy, cynical nod.

"Yep. I guess she knew my old man wasn't going to last very long, so she got out while the going was good. She didn't figger on having to take care of him."

How awful, she wanted to say, but it would sound weak compared to the actual awfulness. "How old were you?"

"Fifteen. Oh, she's still going strong somewhere down Boston way. Sends me a card or a present now and then, if she thinks of it."

"I'm glad you've got your grandparents," she said. "I wish Martin and I had some."

"If she'd run out on us when I was eight or so she'd have done me a favor," he said. "But I was neither hay nor grass. I'd been running free too long, I couldn't set-

145

tle down to being their kid, and besides, I felt real mean most of the time."

"I don't blame you," she said. "You had a reason to feel mean, and I'm sorry. I wish—" But she didn't know what she wished, and began digging in the sand with a big mussel shell.

"Nothing for you to be sorry for," he said dryly. "I know I could be a lot worse off."

Martin came back soon with a handful of flint chips and a new appetite. A thin pearly layer of fog was creeping over the sun, and when they climbed to the top of the island they saw that a band of fog had already hidden the horizon and was dimming the mainland. But there was no chance of being lost between Kestrel and Sea Island, so they dawdled over more food and swam again. None of them was in a hurry to go back. It was the sort of day one wished to go on forever. They were as detached from all that oppressed them as the little island was detached from the mainland, but once the dory's nose touched Sea Island they would no longer be free.

They had to go at last, when the fog began to grow wet and thick in late afternoon. When they came into the cove below Sea House they all three stared round-eyed at what seemed to be an ocean liner looming up in the fog. It turned out to be a smallish cabin cruiser anchored near *Undine*'s mooring, bearing the words *Princess Pat—Port George* on the stern. Some women sitting in the cockpit waved, and the dory passengers waved back.

"Who is it?" Monica asked when Homer shut off the engine.

146

"Oh, summer people. I showed you the house the other day, the one with the long dock." The dory glided with a soft rush of water toward the beach. "Bickmore."

"That's one of the names your grandfather mentioned," said Martin. "That place was broken into." They looked with fresh interest at the stranger who stood on the beach talking with Uncle Theo. He was a trim ruddy-faced man with crewcut white hair. A small varnished pram was pulled up on the sand.

"Ah, here they are!" Uncle Theo hailed them. "My niece and nephew, Monica and Martin Sanborn, and Homer Brice. This is Mr. Bickmore, an old friend of mine from the days when we were your age and even younger."

Mr. Bickmore seemed delighted to meet them, and he knew Homer. "I've seen this young man around town since he was quite a bit smaller. One year he took care of our grass, and nobody's ever done so well since. But I suppose you've outgrown that business, eh?"

Homer grinned bashfully and said nothing. "Bruce heard in town that I was here and he thought it must be my ghost," said Uncle Theo. "He's now discovered the flesh is solid, and he's invited me to dinner."

"I'd like you youngsters to come along with us," said Mr. Bickmore. "All three of you."

"Thanks, Mr. Bickmore," Homer said, "but my grandmother cooked something special for my supper tonight, so I guess I better go along home."

"No, it wouldn't do to disappoint her. But listen, Homer, there are quite a few of us on the Point who'd

147

like someone responsible to look after the lawns and so forth from, say, May till November, and we'd make it worth your while. So think it over, will you?"

"Sure, Mr. Bickmore. Thanks." He pushed off the dory and swung himself in. As the engine started up Mr. Bickmore said regretfully, "I don't suppose he'll consider it. Probably he thinks it's kid stuff now, but we'd pay him a man's wages. Now, how about dinner?"

Monica was tired and not in the mood to be social with strangers, but it was an alternative to an evening with Peter. Unless— "Is Peter going?" she asked politely.

"Peter isn't likely to be back tonight, dear girl. Because of the fog, his mother's plane is to land at Portland, and Peter's borrowed a car and gone to get her. They won't drive back tonight in a dense fog like this one."

"And I may not bring you people home tonight either," said Mr. Bickmore, "but we've plenty of room and we'll like having you."

Martin and Monica didn't need to exchange a glance. She let Martin speak. "Thank you very much, sir," he said formally, "but I think we'd better stay here tonight. I have work that I should have done today, and with the house empty I can really concentrate."

"Great sense of responsibility, these two," Uncle Theo assured Mr. Bickmore, who said he wished his children had showed as much concern for their studies. Uncle Theo went back to the house to change his clothes, and they answered Mr. Bickmore's questions about their European life and their plans for the future. When Uncle Theo returned and the two men prepared to leave, Mr. Bickmore shook hands with them again, warmly.

"It's a great thing to see Sanborns at Sea House again. I hope this is the start of many happy summers for you all."

"Thank you, sir," said Martin, flushing. "Shall I give you a push off?" He waded out and gave the pram a good start across the cove toward *Princess Pat.*

16

"**B**LESS THE FOG," Monica cooed as it pressed ever more thickly and darkly against the windows. With great will power they kept from plunging instantly into the new adventure. They prepared supper and took plenty of time to eat it, expecting that Homer might appear at any time to spend the evening. But as lamplighting time approached they decided to take a stepladder upstairs and have it ready. Martin carried it from the woodshed and through the house, while Monica stood guard at the back door. Still no sign of Homer, and they became fidgety and irritable until Monica had an inspiration.

"I don't think he'll come at all! I'll bet he thinks we've gone with Uncle Theo. Remember, he left right after Mr. Bickmore asked us to dinner."

With his passion for being a secret agent, Martin insisted on their working in the dusk. Time enough to put on a flashlight if and when they got into the locked room.

"If you think anybody's going to be coming in on us, we could lock the outside doors," Monica suggested.

"No, that would look suspicious. What would Mr. Brice think if he should come over here for something?"

"We could say we were afraid of all those ghosts Homer told us about."

Martin frowned at her frivolity. "We'll just have to listen now and then, so as to be sure nobody takes us by surprise. Once we get the trap door open we can lock the sitting room door, so if anyone comes while we're up there they'll simply think that room is kept locked anyway."

"Mr. Brice would know better than that."

"Oh, let's get on with it!" Martin snapped. "Nobody's likely to come, anyway. The Brices know where Homer is because he went home from here, and it's thick as cotton wool outside so nobody, including the burglar, is coming by water."

But by now Monica's elation had died down, she didn't know why. As they set the stepladder in place under the trap door she said gloomily, "With our luck there's a ton of stuff piled on top of it."

"We'll never know till we try." He went up the ladder. "By the pricking of my thumbs, we're about to unloose the Sanborn Monster." Monica laughed, but her heart wasn't in it. Martin placed his hands gently against the door and pushed.

"Sticks a little," he muttered. "It's been painted over. But I think it'll give." In the next instant it gave to the width of about an inch at one end. "Something on it. See if I can slide it off." He kept pushing up on the open end. There was a heavy, slow, sliding sound, and a thump. Martin kept pushing and went up a step at a time on the ladder until his head and shoulders were well into the opening. His long whistle echoed strangely from above.

"What is it?" Monica's heart leaped. "Let me up there!"

151

"Wait till I get things moved around." He grunted and pushed, then said, "All right." He got a knee onto the attic floor and then was all the way into the room and standing up, flashing his light around. As she swung herself up behind him she knew why he'd whistled.

This was indeed the cedar room. There was a dry aromatic fragrance in it, but there was much else, laid around on the floor, set on shelves and boxes and a long table. Binoculars. Cameras. Rifles and shotguns. An elegantly thin portable typewriter in its pale blue case. "Look at this transistor short wave radio," said Martin huskily. "Trans-oceanic."

"Look at *this*," Monica whispered. "A lizard-skin dressing case. Fitted. Here's a pair of cut glass decanters, very old, I'd say." The first wave of shock passed. "Listen, all these things couldn't have *possibly* been in the house here, they've been brought from those mainland places, I'm sure of it. The decanters might belong here, those china spaniels, and maybe the Royal Doulton figurines are here somewhere too, and the set of dueling pistols Uncle Theo was looking for, but—"

"The chess set," said Martin. "Let's look for it." Fascinated, they roamed the long room under the eaves. It was a treasure cave. There was a hodgepodge of small things that must have been stuffed into pockets and taken on the chance they'd bring in some money. Individual crystal salts and peppers with silver caps. Trinkets and ornaments that were no more than inexpensive souvenirs. A couple of jewel boxes held costume jewelry that might or might not have been quite valuable. There were some cashmere sweaters and a man's Irish tweed jacket.

"Look at this." Martin picked up a handful of women's wristwatches. "If they don't take better care of them they'll have nothing to sell." He whistled again. "Our arrival must have really thrown a monkey wrench into the works!" He flashed the light around again, and it illuminated an area behind the lizard-skin case, and showed up the carved lid of the chess box. Monica pounced on it.

"I'm taking this back down. Martin, we have to tell about this now. As soon as the others get here. We know too much, so if we *don't* tell we're accessories."

"Maybe you're right," he said regretfully. "I don't know any way we can catch Pooch short of rigging up a booby trap."

"We've got no time," she said. "No time for anything more. We've got to tell, and then leave. That's all there is to it."

They stood silently in the aromatic room. This was the end of the adventure, all right, and it shouldn't have been so completely depressing. They'd known when they started it that there'd be a letdown at the end. It was just that nothing had been what they'd expected; certainly not this treasure hoard under the eaves.

In the silence they heard a sound. Someone was on the back stairs. Someone was not bothering to be stealthy, and there was more than one someone.

The feeling went out of Monica's hands and feet, and in some queer way out of her head too, so it felt light and

153

ringing. She was still holding the wooden chest, but it had no substance. Martin switched off his light. "Down the ladder!" he whispered fiercely, but she could not move at once. It was like the dreadful paralysis of dreams, and though it only lasted a moment or so it was too long. Someone was unlocking the door.

Here they are, she thought clearly, and we've nothing to stop them with. They could kill us and nobody will know until tomorrow . . . She wished in that instant for Homer to come; for Uncle Theo, even for Peter, nasty little smile or not. "Martin," she whispered, and he stepped around the opening in the floor and stood beside her, facing the door.

As it swung inward a strong light flashed upon them and there was a hissing exclamation behind it. Martin turned his light on the doorway, and they saw Pooch's face, narrowed and knotted together in some odd way, and past his shoulder the yellow blur of Homer's crewcut. *Homer's.*

"You told me they weren't here, you chowderhead," Pooch said hoarsely.

"I thought they were gone." Homer sounded aggrieved. *Homer!* Monica's brain rocked. The two came in, and Pooch set his strong light on end so it filled the low room with an indirect glow. He gave them that grin.

"Couldn't mind your own business, could you? Had to go poking and prying where you'd no right."

"Who's talking about rights?" Martin sounded almost jaunty. "You're a fine one . . . This *is* our business, and

154

we've known about you for quite a while. We wanted clear proof and now we've got it. Of course we didn't know Homer was in it with you. He knew you were in the house the night we found the chess set, didn't he?"

"*Him!*" said Pooch in contempt. "Yeah, he's in it, but I wish I'd thrown him out on his ear a long time ago. I would've, except that this was a perfect place to stash the loot." He lounged against the long table, seeming much at ease. "I told him to get rid of you two prize packages when you first showed up, but he even muffed that."

"What do you mean, get rid of us?" The shock of seeing Homer here had taken away Monica's fear, and she spoke calmly.

"Not to hurt you or anything like that!" Homer broke in. "Just scare you so you'd go away, like the noises the first night and like that time in the fog when you got lost in the woods. That was me whistling all the time, and I yelped and then pushed that old log overboard so you'd think it was him falling. I moved the cover off the well too, but I didn't really think he'd fall into it. I only wanted you to think the place was real spooky and dangerous." He seemed anxious to talk. The words burst out, jerky and breathless. "Afterward I—well, I got to like you after a while, and—"

"Yeah, I had to prod him a mite," said Pooch. "But he couldn't even leave you out on the Mistake for a good chilly night without wrecking his blasted boat."

"That wasn't my fault," Homer defended himself feebly.

"But Homer, we never dreamed you'd do anything

155

like this," said Monica. "This will be terrible for your grandparents. How could you do this to them?"

"They wouldn't ever have to know, if you guys hadn't come barging in!" Homer blustered. "We were going to get everything cleared out before long—we couldn't hide stuff here any longer then, Gramp would be bound to find the locks when he went over the house before fall."

"So that's why you didn't want us to ask about them!" Martin sounded merely interested instead of scared. "Because he didn't know anything about them. You just put them on this summer."

"Sure, and it would have worked out the finest kind. I'd have got my twenty-five horse outboard and more besides."

"With somebody else's property," Monica said softly. "It wouldn't ever have been really yours, Homer, and you know it."

"Why wouldn't it have been mine? Those rich ginks have plenty. *You* have plenty. You two, you've got pots of money behind you, so you can stand there and say, Oh, it's wrong, it's stealing—"

"You can stop right there, Homer," said Monica. "We haven't got pots of money. We haven't anything except for a little money from insurance to pay for our food and clothes till we're on our own. If we want to go to college we'll have to work for scholarships."

"La-di-da!" said Pooch. "Don't she talk some fancy now? Homer thought she was some nice, didn't you, Homer? He sure loves the elegant kind of talking. It almost caught him. He was some moony-eyed for a

156

while." The grin, Monica thought, was positively loathsome. "I could go for her myself," he went on, "except that she thinks she's too good for me. Well, now we'll see who's too good for who."

"You'd better watch it, Pooch," said Martin, desperately quiet about it. Pooch laughed, and Martin flung his flashlight at him. It hit the other boy a glancing blow on the shoulder. Pooch got up and came leisurely toward him, bringing his hand out from behind his back. It held one of the cut-glass decanters by the neck. As he swung his arm up the glass flashed beautifully in the light and then it swung down toward Martin's skull, but before it hit, Homer plunged forward and grabbed Pooch around the waist in a perfect tackle. The decanter flew, and Pooch crashed against Martin, who jumped backward and bumped into Monica. The chess set flew out of her hands and showered down through the hole into the sitting room, and Homer fell through at the same time. He cried out in strangled fright, the stepladder collapsed, and then there was a heart-stopping silence from the dark room below.

"If he's dead, Pooch," Martin said in a voice of doom, "it's your fault."

Pooch scrambled to his feet and ran with his head down toward the door. Martin started after him around the trap door opening. Monica tried to hold him back, but her fingers closed on air. "Let him go!" she cried. "We've got to see about Homer!"

There was a grunting collision in the doorway, but Martin wasn't involved. He seized Pooch's light and

157

turned it on the wrestling mass. Peter's face showed clear for a moment, set with strain, and then Martin handed the light to his sister, saying grimly, "Keep it out of our eyes."

Pooch had fought clear of Peter for an instant and was fumbling inside his jacket when Martin jumped on his back. Something bounced out of Pooch's hand and clattered on the stairs. Peter swooped it up. It was so small Monica could hardly see it but she knew by the way Peter held it that it was a gun.

"Thanks, Martin," he said, slightly out of breath. "You can let him go. He won't go anywhere." Released, Pooch sagged against the door, staring at Peter's hand as if at a poisonous snake preparing to strike. Martin was winded but jubilant. Down in the sitting room another light flashed on, and Uncle Theo's dry voice said, "Young man, what are you doing sitting there amid my chess set? . . . No, you had better sit there and nurse your bruises. Perhaps I should warn you that I have been an instructor in hand-to-hand fighting for guerilla troops. Judo, karate, all sorts of low tricks."

Then in a different voice he said, "Bless my soul, it's Homer!"

17

DOWN IN the lamplit kitchen Pooch and Homer sat side by side, Pooch glaring at the floor, Homer looking everywhere but at Monica and Martin, who in turn did not want to look at him. A fire burned in the black iron range, the teakettle sang, there was an appetizing scent of fresh coffee. A tall woman with dark red hair twisted gracefully at the back of her head was giving first aid to Homer's scrapes and bruises. Peter sat on a corner of the table with his arms folded. Uncle Theo had gone to get Mr. Brice.

"It's going to be difficult for that poor chap and for his wife too. I hope they won't think they have to leave . . . I may be able to help a little, just by being someone their own age to talk with . . . I don't know." Shaking his head, he had departed.

Sometime during the early investigation of the cedar room the wind had whipped briskly around to the northwest and blown the fog away. "We'd got to Port George by dusk," the tall woman said, "and when it cleared— well, after all these years I couldn't endure the thought of spending the night ashore if there was a way to reach Sea Island. So my invaluable son discovered a man going out to look for herring, and he dropped us off here."

"The invaluable Mont Cady," said Peter with a smile, not nasty but rather bemused. "Uncle Theo must have

159

been put ashore in the cove just about the time we reached the house."

"I'm glad everybody did come," Monica said huskily.

"So am I." Peter touched the little automatic on the table. "Did you two have an idea what was up there?"

"Not really," Martin said, "but we knew somebody had been up there. And we knew some things had disappeared from the house, like the chess set. But Monica didn't find the trap door till the day before yesterday."

"We weren't going to leave without telling you about it," said Monica. "But we did want to see what was up there."

"Naturally," said the woman with a faint smile. "I would have wanted to see myself. Did you say you were leaving?"

Burning, Monica still managed to gaze straight at her. "Yes. It's time for us to go." She was glad that Uncle Theo came in then, but not glad to see Mr. Brice. And there was no time to go into another room.

Homer turned a deep scarlet from his throat to his temples. Monica had never felt so sorry for anyone in her life, even though she knew he deserved this discomfort, unless it was for Mr. Brice. He stood looking bleakly at his grandson, then recalled his manners and nodded at Peter's mother.

"How'd you do . . . Come on, Homer." The dogs bounded in past him and were so glad to see everyone that their joy made the gloom seem that much darker. Babe put her head in Monica's lap for a moment, George laughed at her with flopping tongue and topaz eyes, and then they were gone to swarm all over Pooch and Homer, who ignored them.

"We all go over in the morning in my boat, then," Mr. Brice said to Uncle Theo, who nodded. Homer got up like a sleepwalker. Pooch spoke for the first time, twisting his mouth as if he tasted something vile.

"Cheer up, chum, Gramp'll get you off. There's nobody to give a darn what happens to *me*."

"You're wrong, Pooch," said Mr. Brice. "I won't try to get Homer off, even if I thought I could do it. He'll take what's coming to him and profit by it, I hope."

Martin cleared his throat. "Homer jumped Pooch when Pooch was going to brain me with a heavy glass decanter. That's how Homer fell through the trap door."

Everybody but Pooch looked at Homer with new interest, tinged with kindness. He went out quickly with the dogs, and his grandfather followed. It was very quiet for a few moments, and then Uncle Theo said as to himself, "Too bad, too bad."

"I guess we'd better lock this one away for the night," said Peter. "Monica, how about making up the bed in that small room next to mine?"

"Of course." She was eager to move. "Give me your light, Martin . . . After I do that I guess I'll go to bed."

"I'm going right now." Martin was also in a hurry to escape.

"Please, both of you," said Peter's mother. "Come back to the kitchen and have a hot drink. We all need to calm down and try to think." It was gentle enough, but it was a command.

Martin helped make up the bed, though she didn't

161

really need help. Neither had much to say. Was the night dream or nightmare? Had it been only a few hours ago, or a lifetime, when they'd wandered the shores of Kestrel and murmured in the sun? Again the shattering unreality of seeing Homer there with Pooch in the attic hit Monica, this time in the stomach. In an effort to steady herself she said, "Did you hear Uncle Theo say he'd taught judo and karate and things like that to guerilla troops?"

"*What?* No, and you never did either. Your brain must have been disordered from shock, or something."

"I did too hear him. And I believe him. It's just insane enough to be true."

"Insane is the right word . . . Do you want to go back down there with them?"

"No, but we're outnumbered."

Martin groaned. "I shouldn't have any sympathy for Homer, but right now I do."

"Well, at least we can look neat," said Monica in an older-sister tone. They went to their rooms to comb their hair and otherwise tidy up, then went sedately down to the kitchen. Uncle Theo and Peter escorted a silent Pooch out of the room. Mrs. Sanborn made light talk about her memories of the stove and the kitchen, and from habit Monica set out cups and saucers. Peter's mother was warming cinnamon rolls in the oven.

"I brought them all the way from New York because my son likes them," she said. "This special kind, I mean. Makes me sound terribly sentimental, doesn't it? But I thought he deserved something for inviting his mother to spend the weekend with him."

Monica tried to smile, and murmured, "I'll cut some butter."

"Let me take that flashlight, Martin," Peter's mother said. "I'd like to look around a bit while they're securing Pooch . . . He must have another name. If he hasn't, that one must have driven him to crime . . ." She went off and left them and they looked at each other in bleak, exhausted silence. Everything was being drawn out to an unbearably fine point.

Peter and Uncle Theo returned, not exactly cheerful but with an air of accomplishment. "He can't go anywhere from that window," said Peter. "There's nothing to go down by, and there's a sheer drop to that granite outcropping below." He turned to Martin. "You did all right, climbing his frame like that. His little shooting iron there is loaded and all ready to go. So—many thanks."

"You're welcome," said Martin, distantly.

Peter's mother came back into the room. She had a swift long-legged stride which Monica would have admired under different circumstances. "They've managed to get the Lowestoft away from here. Who do you suppose told them it was valuable?"

Monica felt herself blushing as if she, not Uncle Theo, had hidden the rare porcelain. *Would* he let the boys take the blame for it?

"Oh, maybe it wasn't here at all," said Mrs. Sanborn. "I'd heard that Madam left it, but perhaps she changed her mind and sent for it."

Monica tried not to stare at Uncle Theo and was sure that she looked immensely guilty herself. It would be an

163

easy out for him to pretend Madam *had* sent for the porcelain. She tingled unpleasantly with suspense. Across the room Uncle Theo said, "Oh—er—you've seen the—er—Lowestoft, have you? You must have—er—come into the family after I—er—left. I haven't been able to place you—your son—er—has been rather vague—"

Suddenly his whole manner became sharp and bright, like the weather when the fog blew away. "Oh, let's have an end to this tomfoolery," he said harshly. "No, Madam didn't send for the Lowestoft, and the boys didn't make away with it. It's up in my room, packed in a trunk. I was going to take it with me and sell it.

"Are you broke, Theo?" she asked softly.

"*Broke* is no word for it! I'm rolled out as flat as a caterpillar run over by a steam roller. Big business on one hand and my wife's long illness on the other. I've always been thankful I could take care of her as I did. My company didn't merge with a giant and throw some of us into the cold until she was safely out of it. But to make a new start at my age—" he gave them all a cheerful, reckless smile. "Good Lord, I could barely pay my rent! I began dreaming like a hungry man of that porcelain sitting here, gathering dust. Someone could be using that stuff and adoring it, and I could be using and adoring the money. I can see now that it won't work. I wonder if Bruce Bickmore and his friends would be willing to hire a boy of my age as their gardener."

Everybody laughed to help him out. "Seriously," he said, "Brice tells me there's always a shortage of teachers around here. I have the education and I think, though I may be vain, the knack. I'm going to see the proper people at Augusta." He gave them all that charming smile. "At least I've been thinking about it since I realized I hadn't the stomach for absconding with the Lowestoft—even though the waste of it still appalls me.

"I think you'd make a marvelous teacher, Uncle Theo," Monica blurted out.

"*I'd* like to go to school to you, sir," said Martin handsomely.

"Thank you, dear children."

"Congratulations on your decision, Theo," said Mrs. Sanborn. "I'm sure you'll have no difficulty. They should grab you up at once. And speaking of the Lowestoft, it's ridiculous to let things drift on like this year after year. This house should be *used* at least in summer. A whole generation of youngsters are being cheated out of their birthright, to say nothing of us older ones who always loved it so. I think an immense all-out effort should be made to contact all the heirs and force a settlement of the estate."

"You still haven't told me who you are." Uncle Theo was frowning at her. "Arthur's grandson's wife? Edward's daughter-in-law?"

She smiled at him. "You sent me your blessing once, Theo, and I've always loved you for it."

His mouth opened, his eyes widened, then delight blazed across his face. "You're *Lydia!* Tom's Lydia! Then—" Bewildered, he turned to Martin and Monica. It was the moment they hadn't intended ever to let

165

happen. Feeling like Pooch and Homer, they didn't move.

"Yes, children," said Mrs. Sanborn gently. "This may come as a shock to you, but I'm your mother."

Hold your head up, Monica silently ordered her brother. Look them all straight in the face. "Our father and mother were Mark and Ellen Christie," she said.

"I've heard of Mark Christie," said Peter. "He was Dad's best friend all the time they were growing up." He was not disagreeable, but interested, and that was worse; it was like being placed under a microscope. Monica lifted her head higher. Martin spoke in a remarkably steady and mature manner.

"Sea Island and Sea House meant America to us. It was the place we wanted to see most. We thought our father'd had the best growing-up a kid could have, being able to come to Sea Island in the summers."

"I remember you two!" Peter broke in suddenly. "Martin was a very solemn baby in the playpen, and you were about a foot tall," he said to Monica. "At least you seemed that little to me. You could run around under tables, and were you fast! My sister thought you were some kind of live doll, and she started demanding a little sister as soon as we left." He laughed. "Where in heck was that, Mother?"

"In Paris, before we moved back to the States. We saw a lot of Mark and Ellen in those days." She studied the two thoughtfully. "When Simon called and told me I had two children here that I'd never laid eyes on, I never guessed. I couldn't imagine who they'd be, and it was so fantastic I could only laugh like an idiot and say I'd come right away. But the minute I saw those dark eyes, I knew."

"*You're* Simon?" Martin gazed at Peter. "You're supposed to be in the Army."

"I go next month. And I'm Simon Peter—or Simon Pure, as my sister likes to insult me ... That time in Paris I made these ghoulish faces at you and you never blinked. But *you* were fascinated," he said to Monica. "It went to my head."

"He got quite drunk with his own charm," said his mother. "His father had to practically sit on him."

"Why didn't you call the police about us?" Monica asked politely, looking from Simon to his mother. They seemed to be so amused, so quick to laugh, that she was confused. Her head was beginning to ache.

"Well, neither of us thought you were a pair of infant-prodigy criminals," said Mrs. Sanborn, "being sought by Interpol and all that."

"But I have to admit I thought you were a couple of smooth-talking deadly little brats," said Simon. "A pair of highly intelligent juvenile delinquents who'd heard about the place here in some roundabout way and talked themselves in, and would move out with your luggage full of everything it would hold."

Monica's face burned. Even her eyes were on fire. But she would not blink them, or lower her head. Mrs. Sanborn said in a soft, almost dreaming voice, "Yes, he was furious when he called me. Then we walked into this— this crisis, and then, when it was over, into the lamplight came Mark and Ellen's children." Her faint smile was not for them; she seemed to be looking past them into another time. "As I told you when I wrote, your parents were involved with the happiest years of my life."

Monica put her hand up to her dry and aching throat, was able to swallow, and said, "I think we should explain. We finished out our school year in Paris, staying in our flat there. Then these French friends of our family saw us off for home. It was two weeks earlier than Aunt Naomi expected us, but we let the Chevaliers think we'd wired her." Then her voice gave out altogether, for lack of breath. Martin spoke firmly.

"We were going to steal two weeks. We didn't know if we'd ever get near Sea Island, but we thought maybe we could hire someone to take us out around it so we could see it. Everyone took us for Tom Sanborn's son and daughter. We didn't say it in the first place, we didn't mean to lie, it just seemed to happen." After a moment he said, "We should have stopped it."

"Martin wanted to," Monica broke in, "but I talked him out of it. I didn't think we'd do any harm. I told him we deserved this adventure." It seemed as if this hour had been going on forever, and there was nothing to do but plow doggedly ahead through the morass of shame and embarrassment. "You used to send us things Simon and Anne had outgrown. When we wore them we played we *were* Simon and Anne. We used to think being a Sanborn meant being born lucky, because of Sea House."

"I see," Lydia Sanborn said. Simon was staring at the floor, and Uncle Theo fussed with his pipe.

"So that's it," Monica finished. "We'll go in the morning when Pooch and Homer go, unless you want to have us arrested too. Come on, Martin."

A curious stillness surrounded them as they stood up. Then Simon said after them, "Listen, you two put a stop to the thievery here. We won't forget that."

"Thank you," said Monica. They left the kitchen and went side by side up the stairs, separated in silence, and went to their rooms. Passing the door behind which Pooch waited for morning Monica thought, You go to the sheriff and we go to Aunt Naomi. How about changing places?

In her room she lit her lamp and undressed, then began picking up her belongings. When she got through, she'd go to see her brother, and they might be able to talk a little and help each other out.

They needed a lot of bolstering now, and the worst of it was that this simply wasn't one hard spot to get over. Life with Aunt Naomi lay ahead, made worse by the taunting memories of Sea Island. She could hardly bear to look around her at the gracious room in which she had found such security for a little while. It would have been better for her and her brother, she thought drearily, if their father had not relived with them so much of his golden boyhood in this house.

There was a tap at the door and she expected Martin. "Come in," she said in a dull voice. The door opened, and Martin was there all right, giving her a shaky little grin, but so was Peter's mother. She carried a tray and Martin pushed things aside on a table to make room for it.

169

"You went off without trying my special *café au lait* and cinnamon rolls," she said briskly. "So I came after you, and picked up your brother on the way. Now sit down, both of you, and drink while it's hot. I'll have a cup with you. I want to talk."

"What is there to say," asked Monica, "unless you want to tell us that we're as dishonest as Pooch and Homer?"

Lydia Sanborn was unruffled. "Yes, it was dishonest, but you didn't intend to take anything that wasn't yours; only to borrow it for a little while, I think, and return it as good as new. I can see why you did, and I don't think I blame you. But nothing is ever as simple as it appears to be, nothing is ever completely on the surface." She poured hot milk and hot coffee as if she were presiding at some elegant social occasion. "Because of your act *you* are changed, and Theo is changed. My life and Simon's and his sister's are changed. Sea House is going to come alive again. You stopped the robberies, perhaps you've saved Homer's future for him, though I can't make any guesses about Pooch. You kept Theo from getting into trouble by taking the Lowestoft. Simon wouldn't have come to the island at all if he hadn't heard at Port George that Tom Sanborn's children were here." She smiled at them. "Please drink that while it's hot and see if it makes you think of Paris. And try not to be embarrassed. The time for that is past."

"It will never be past," said Monica.

"I'm older, and I *know*. . . . I also knew your Aunt Naomi, briefly. When we came back to the States so long ago I went to see her, to let her know how Mark was get-

170

ting along. I was young then, and intolerant, and there were a good many things I didn't understand. When I met her this spring, it was like meeting a different person, because I had grown older and a bit wiser."

"She doesn't like us," Monica explained, not bitterly but as if stating a simple fact of life. "She loathes us."

"No, she doesn't. She's afraid of you."

Both Martin and Monica sat up straighter, faces stiff with disbelief. "I don't understand," said Monica faintly. "Why should she be afraid of us? We'll be in her power, not she in ours."

"She's not a wicked witch out of a fairy tale," said Mrs. Sanborn dryly. "And you two aren't exactly Hansel and Gretel . . . She said to me, 'If they are as united as Mark and I were once, I won't exist for them except as something barely to be tolerated.' She's a very lonely woman, and right now an apprehensive one, but she's very proud too. She only told me that because she was so shaken up at the time."

"She and my father were *close?* I don't get it," said Martin flatly. "Why didn't she ever show it?"

"She did, by her hurt silence. When he went to Paris she expected him to come back, but he married there and he didn't come back. It was not right for her to center her life on him, but it was very human. She knows now what it did to her. And she's terrified of his children." She looked from one pair of dark eyes to the other. "I wouldn't tell you this about her, and abuse her confidence, except that I think you're both exceptionally fair-minded and you won't take advantage of her."

171

Martin stirred his drink, frowning at it. But Monica was gazing into the past, hearing her father's voice. *Be close to your brother always, but don't live for him and don't let him live for you. You've each got your own way to choose and travel. The earlier you realize that, the less you'll wound and be wounded.*

The moment was so real, the voice so warm, that she wanted to bow her head and cry helplessly for the safe and loving world of the past. But through grief came the ring of truth, a warning bell through fog. So that's what he meant! she thought. He knew what he was saying.

Martin cleared his throat and said sternly, "I see that the situation isn't quite cut-and-dried."

"No family relationship ever is," said Mrs. Sanborn. "Look at the tangle in this house, for instance, and what old Mrs. Sanborn suffered. She *did* suffer, believe me, but she wouldn't let anyone help her, she just kept striking out and hitting everyone within reach. It was a long reach too," she added. "Tom never stopped loving her. Well, that's all in the past now." She got up and walked around the room, looking at the photographs and water colors. What is she thinking? Monica wondered, remembering guiltily that this house was full of memories for Lydia Sanborn . . . The woman turned back to them and smiled.

"When you go to her, will you try to make it work?" she asked. "Meet her halfway, or go even farther, because you have so much more on your side, youth and flexibility, and your lives ahead of you. It won't be heaven, but you can make it endurable, and maybe a little better than that . . . You'll be free to visit me now and then, I'm pretty sure, and that will give you all a breathing space."

Martin didn't move. He had folded his hands on the edge of the table and sat staring down at them. Monica said, "Thank you for telling us about her. Father never had much to say. I guess—I *think* I know why now. If they'd been really close as children, it would have been hard later to have her so hurt and upset, and—and unforgiving."

Mrs. Sanborn nodded. "You see, you're already beginning to understand. Drink your *café au lait* and go to bed, and try to sleep. Tomorrow's going to be a hard day." She turned to the door, and Martin jumped up and went to open it for her.

"Good night," he and Monica said together. When the door shut behind her he leaned against the panels and blew hard. "What are you thinking?"

"I can't sort it all out now. There's too much. Just one thing is sure—we're in her debt. We can't do anything else but what she asks, and she knows it. She's as certain of us right now as if we'd sworn a blood oath."

"And you know something?" asked Martin. "She's got a right to be. We owe her plenty." His grin was weary but full of courage and gaiety. "Practically half our future, if we get a chance to come back to Sea House."

"Not to mention an aunt," said Monica. "Just think, what if we'd gone to Aunt Naomi not knowing, and all of us with huge chips on our shoulders?"

"Sounds murderous," said Martin cheerfully. He sat down at the table and picked up a cinnamon roll. "Fall in, men! Let's eat."

173

About the Author

Elisabeth Ogilvie, well-known novelist, is the author of six other books for young people, *Becky's Island, Blueberry Summer, Ceiling of Amber, How Wide the Heart, Turn Around Twice, The Young Islanders,* and *Whistle for a Wind,* and many adult books including *The Witch Door, High Tide at Noon, Storm Tide, The Ebbing Tide,* and *The Dawning of the Day.*

Born, raised, and educated in Massachusetts, Miss Ogilvie decided upon two things while still in high school: to be an author and to live in Maine. An island in the mouth of the historic St. George River, below Thomaston, is her year-round home. Her hobbies, which keep her busy when she is not writing, are boats, reading, music, and—of course—Maine.